Seven More Lives for Felix the Tomcat

(Felix the Tomcat Part 2)

Felix the Tomcat

And M. P. Frank

"Don't you wish you had a job like mine. All you have to do is sit around and think up a certain number of words. You can repeat words... and they don't have to be TRUE!"
—Dave Barry

Disclaimer

This book is a work of fiction. Any names, characters, companies, organizations, places, events, locales, and incidents are either used in a fictitious manner or are fictional. Any resemblance to actual persons, living or dead, actual companies or organizations, or actual events is purely coincidental.

ISBN 978-1-7388165-3-8

For rights and permissions, please contact:

Michael Patrick Frank and Felix the Tomcat

Michealpatrickfrankwriter@gmail.com

Thanks

To my incredible friends…my gang… Slick, Goldenboy, Hank, Gloomer, Rosa, lovely Afrodite…. And even that asshole V- Dome.   Sincerely, Felix the Tomcat

To my amazing partner, Linda, and my loyal friends and family, and my amazing four grandkids. I hope someday, when your parents let you read this, you will chuckle and say, "Wow, Pop was a trip!" Thank you to Joseph Idaye at Upwork for formatting this book and designing the cover for Kindle.   M.P. Frank

See our website: FelixtheTomcat2022.blog/

Please write a review on Amazon.ca or Amazon.com

Or write it and mail it to:

Michaelpatrickfrankwriter@gmail.com

All reviews welcomed and appreciated.

To the Reader

Thank you for reading this book. We hope you enjoyed reading it as much as we enjoyed dreaming it up. Please leave an honest book review at Amazon.com or Amazon.ca. Thank you for your support.

The Authors: M.P. Frank and that rascal, Felix the Tomcat

Humor is the juxtapositifying of the incongruous. —Felix the Tomcat

A day without laughter is a day wasted. —Charlie Chaplin

Sometimes I wonder if this is all happening because I didn't forward that email to ten people.

We don't stop playing because we get old; we grow old because we stop playing. —George Bernard Shaw

Table of Contents

Chapter 1

Heaven Sent

"Go to heaven for the climate; go to hell for the company."—Mark Twain

When we regained consciousness, me and Slick were in front of the Pearly Gates. Amazingly, the gates didn't fall over because the gateposts were just stuck in the clouds. Me and Slick also looked unstable on our feet. Slick looked like he had been eaten or severely chewed up. I was the same… a lot of bite marks and what I assumed was coyote spit.

Slick said, "The goddam coyote got us. Killed us both Dead-Dead!" I said, "Slick, we are screwified. Our math in the 'lives spent' column was faultified."

An old man with curly white hair and a big white beard and bushy eyebrows, wearing a white choir gown outfit (but no wings) shuffled over to us.

"Hi, guys, I am Saint Pete Junior, but you can call me St. Pete. Welcome to the Pearly Gates. What are your names?"

I said, "I am Felix the Tomcat, from Pittsburg."

Slick said, "Slick."

St. Pete chuckled, "A little trouble with a coyote. I hear."

I said, "Indeed."

Slick said, "Fucking coyote."

St. Pete said, "Come on in and take a load off. Hope you didn't miss supper." St. Pete spoke decent Catonese (the universal cat language.)

Using the hem of St. Pete's white gown to wipe coyote spit from what used to be my purrfect white, black, orange and brown rossetified fur I replied, "We were supper. Goddam Coyote supper!"

St. Pete led us into a fancy, pure white reception hall with a buffet supper and comfy sofas.

St. Pete said, "Sorry, fellows we are slammed. God is in rehab for a decade in the Alpha Centauri Galaxy. He got into the sauce bigly and also developed PTFSD

(Post Traumatic Fucking Stress Disorder). 'Being God' got to be way too much stress for him, with Covid and Putin and that asshole, Rump, and don't get me started on that new Webb telescope in space. Cosmologists have already discovered another 50 trillion galaxies for us to manage. All our good help left. Jesus went back to carpentry... union job in Vegas. Mary is off on maternity leave... triplets. Ai-Yi-Yi! I got this 'bouncer job' online on 'Glassdoor.'"

I said, 'What happened to the traditional gatekeeper, Old St. Peter?

St. Pete chuckled, "He got tired of all the bullshit after a million years on the job. He quit 50 years ago and got reincarnated as Dwayne Johnson... you know,' The Rock'... wrestler, football player, actor, chick magnet. He is loving the celebrity life."

He stabbed a finger in the direction of the giant white 'Book of Life,' and muttered, "We are still friggin' analog! The paperwork is Hell. Some Idiot sentenced Steve Jobbers to Purgatory for 84,000 years! We could have used that guy to straighten out our records."

I said, "Who is in charge? Who decides our fate now that both of us are Dead-Dead?"

St. Pete smiled, "At the moment, we have accommodations for Buddists only."

He winked twice at me and Slick. Then Pete shook his head, "Christians are all heading to Purgatory for at least 50,000 years till we train some new staff. Gonna be a bad few decamillenia fo Christians."

I said, "Me and Slick are bonafidified Buddists... Namaste, Pete."

Slick gave a thumbs up. St. Pete nodded. We hit the buffet for some excellent fish, bacon and cream served to us by guys with wings and T-shirts saying, "Wings to Go." The harp orchestra was playing Billy Joel and Elton John tunes. St. Pete sang 'Candle in the Wind' in harmony with himself. Slick and me sang our now famous rendition of 'Crying" by Roy Orbison. It was hard to wail with your throat ripped open, but we did our best.

After dessert, we got paged, "Felix and Slick to the Buddist Golden Chamber." We followed the golden line on the floor to a cavernous door which opened as we walked up.

There, sitting on a golden throne, with gold cushions, was old Budda. You remember Budda: fat, saffron robe, chubby face... always happy. You remember he ate a canary in 'Nine Lives.' (My first book.)

Anyway, Budda looked at us, "Hmmm. A coupla troublemakers... called Felix and Slick. What's up?"

He spoke good Catonese. I stammered, "We tried to be good. Really."

Old Budda was in hysterics, "I love it! What a job! Bullshit 24/7!"

He continued to chuckle, giving his knee a good slap every few seconds. Finally, he got more serious and peered at us.

"Look fellas, this whole place is slammed. Tell you what… you agree to do 9 more lives on Earth and try harder… I will throw in new bodies."

Slick finally said something, "Five lives, with go-nads. That is my final offer."

I said, "I want to be a jaguar. Seven lives."

Budda howled, "And I want to be Brad Pitt!"

Budda looked serious, "Ok, boys. Here is the deal. You are going back to earth as Tomcats… with go-nads. Seven more lives. New bodies… just like the originals. Back to Pittsburg… who needs a Hell when you have Pittsburg?"

We high-fived on the deal. I raised a few more issues, "Budda, me and Slick would like to lodge a Karma request to be directed against that odious coyote, who ate us."

Budda punched a few numbers into the intercom phone keypad built into his golden throne and turned on the speaker,"

"Hey, Shirley, Budda here. Could you buzz me the Department of Corrective Karma. I need the operative for North Suburban Branch Office in Pitttsburg. He drummed his chubby fingers on the golden arm of his throne.

"Howdy." Said a voice, "Ya got Fred in Karma Corrections -North Pittsburg Branch Office."

"Got a coyote killing cats again in Pittsburg." Said Budda.

Fred said, 'It's that fucking Willie Coyote, back from Arizona again. That dude is just bad. And he keeps ordering machines and rocket shit on Amazon. What kind of Karma have ya got in mind, Budda?"

Budda smiled tolerantly and said, "Ship him back to Casa Grande, Arizona and cancel his Amazon Prime membership and his credit card. Let him chase that friggin road runner for few centuries, on foot!"

Budda smiled at us and asked, "Boys, where is your 'Happy Place', on Earth? After your resurrection I will send you there to live out your seven new lives."

Budda pointed to the entrance of a cave stuck in the cloud two hundred yards away, "That is the resurrection chamber. Jesus did a reno on it before he took off for Vegas. Been right there ever since Lazarus… but it still works great. Me and Slick shared a skeptified glance.

Old Mother Teresa was standing outside the cave, dressed in her habitual blue and white robes, smoking a stogie. Her face was seriously wrinkled and suntanned. "Hi boys. Little trouble with a coyote, I hear. I am working part-time on the Resurrectifyer... the Pope cut my pension with all the lawsuits and shit. A girl has gotta eat."

She showed us the way into the spooky cave and we had to lie down on big stone slabs. She covered us up with pieces of linen called shrowds and looked at me 'Felix, this shrowd could be worth big money on Ebay if you actually get on Opa Windfree."

Anyway, they soon rolled a big rock into place to seal the cave and it became black as coal. I had to pee. I groped my way around the cavern, using my trusty whiskers. Cats have 24 whiskers around the mouth called mystacial vibrissae and extra whiskers above the eyes and on the back of the forelegs. Whiskers act as sensory antennas to plot the distance, direction and surface texture of objects near the cat them... like bat radar. Thank god for whiskers.

Soon we heard a rumble and the cave shook, like a tank just drove by outside. A strange creeping warmth started in my ears and worked its way all through my body down to my back paws and the tip of my flat tail. A few minutes later, the stone got rolled back and Slick and me jumped to our feet and strode back into the heavenly gathering chamber. A Moreman choir in golden gowns was singing Handel's 'Hallelujah Chorus.' Me and Slick did some Irish Jig dancing to show off our new robustified, ressurectified bodies. I loved my new round tail and my new intact ears. Slick had all his teeth. We carefully checked that we both had our go-nads.

Slick gave me a happy grin, "Dynamite, Pardner."

I whooped, "Ya betcha, Baby!"

We had seven more lives and we were feelin fine.

Chapter 2

Back in Pittsburg

"One loyal friend is worth 10,000 relatives."—Euripedes

Me and Slick were sitting in the crotch of our favorite maple tree at 1 PM. (Our Happy Place). Slick could not resist performing an acrobatic pirouette to snafu a Baltimore oriol that had forgotten to fly south. Slick leaped and twisted like a teenager. We shared the oriol who, as a food group, are nothing special... mostly feathers. Catapulting out of the tree I did some speed laps around the meadow and caught a small Jack rabbit. We snacked on our prey. Slick and me planned to meet up after dark to get back into mousing and ratting and pregnifying some horny Queens. Life pumped through our new bodies like we were kittens-this was Quality!

I headed back to the manshun, entering the sunroom through the catflap. I stopped in the mudroom to admire myself in the mirror… my brand new whole ears and my new non-flat gorgeous white, brown, orange tail with black rosettes. Rosa had left me some cream and tuna fish. I loved Rosa.

I planned to snooze till the teenagers got home from school. Goldenboy and Gloomer arrived home about 4 PM. They were chatting with Rosa… in Spanish. Goldenboy was sharing our misadventures at the Sinus fair and Rosa and Gloomer howled with laughter. He was impersonating Dr. Nuts with her twitches and ?Tourettes. Goldenboy and me hired a publicity agent… on Amazon to field the all the offers we were receiving. So far, I agreed to three nights in Vegas to do a standup open on Tenn and Peller and a special interview with Opa Windfree on "How smart are cats? Do they have a sense of humor?"

The Pope had invited us to Rome for a visit and to perform some stand-up for the College of Cardinals. The Pope had taken a pro-Felix stance because of my insistence on preserving my sperm for procreation. He also approved of me trashing all the other faiths. My first book, 'The Nine Lives of Felix the Tomcat,' was coming along swimmingly… I was up to 35000 words. I had taken an advance from Penguin Random House for $25,000, most of which I put in Goldenboy's college fund.

Random House expected me to finish and publish the story of my adventures and my first nine lives within a month. I could easily spit out 1000 words a day… hell, it was my life. My new editor was a suck-up who fully appreciated my witified prose. I also needed a new laptop and a color printer. I was a Tomcat with an agenda. Gloomer was excited and supportive of Goldenboy and me.

Rosa said, "Ustedes son la bomba!" (You guys are the bomb!" Rosetta's stones.)

Editor's Note: Felix… you arrogant asshat. I am not a suck-up. You wanna see the dark side?

Arthurs Note: No thanks. I like this side. I just mean you are nice and helpful, so far.

Editor's Note: And who is the suck-up now?

I helped Goldenboy service and feed his menagerie. Goldenboy managed a huge collection of rare and tropical birds and beasts in realistic woodland conditions in his huge bedroom complex (the size of a Seven-Eleven). He had a 7 foot red-tailed Boa called Bo, four tarantulas (defanged) with 9 inch leg-spans, 40 Salt-water fish (Salties), a dozen foot-long iguanas and lizards, and a pair of parakeets called Lewis and Quark, who called me and Goldenboy, "Handsome." I snafued two white mice from the basement mouse farm when we went down to get supper for Bo the Boa.

In my research, I discovered that cats cannot develop clinical Hankyvirus (Google)… but they can get Toxoplasmosis from eating raw rodents.

Cats are the prime carrier of Toxoplasmosis Gandhi, which contaminates soil (and litterboxes) when they poop. The rodents catch it from cat feces and the cats catch it back from the rodents , if they eat them. (Karma in action.) Toxoplasmosis can be serious in cats: lethargy, fever, weight loss, depression, seizures, and even death.

Cats can pass Toxo to human babies with devastating effects, including blindness. So, what do the experts advise? Keep your damn cat inside. (See Chapter 26 'The Nine Lives of Felix the Tomcat' for my rant on this subject.) The other advice is to keep your damn infants out of your cat's litterbox. (duh!)

Night fell and I headed out for a night of adventure with Slick. We were enjoying our relative youth and feeling very frisky. Slick was meowing 'Memories' from 'Cats' when I arrived at our Happy Place. He believed he had a good tenor voice. We chatted for a while, then headed off for some serious mousing and ratting at the leaky granary. The word was out among the barn cats was that 'Willie the Coyote' had disappeared in a 'Rapture-type' event in the middle of the night. I was completely sold on Buddism and was a solid believer in the Department of Corrective Karma. (North Pittsburg Branch Office)

Me and Slick had a grand time chasing, killing and eating field mice and a few rats. Our youthful new bodies were amazing. We were unstoppable. No owls and no coyotes bothered us. Slick had all his teeth again and beautiful unmangled slick pointy ears. He was a stud again. On the subject of studdism, we set a new Guinness Sleep Safe Trailer Park Coitus record.... twelve hornified Queens serviced (royally) in one night... six each. We loved our newly spermified go-nads... the Pope should be proud. We were whipped and had a good sleep on the flat metal roof of the trailer.

As the sun rose, I crept back through the cat-flap for some serious shut-eye. Rosa had left me a bowl of cream.

Chapter 3

Hank goes Electric and Sven has a Ball

"Let's put the fun back in Dysfunctional."—Anon

I slept like a kitten for the morning. The door bell woke me up. Goldenboy had hooked my iPad into the security system… so I could open the door for my Amazon deliveries.

When the door opened, the Amazon driver was none other than Hank, wearing a blue and black Amazon outfit, including a ballcap with a swooshed arrow. Slick stood beside him, wearing a matching uniform with his ball cap on backwards. (extra-small Blue and black)

Slick was on his hind legs, leaning on the door jamb, smoking a pipe.

I said, "Slick, I thought you quit smoking."

Slick said, "Nope."

Hank was driving a brand spanking-new all-electric Amazon delivery van.

He said, "Helluva gig, Felix. This is fun. No more greasy spoon truckstops for this guy. Just delivering shit to people with too much shit."

He pointed at Slick, "Hired my own assistant."

Slick said, "My first job-job," and shook his head. He was a tomcat. We tomcats had a work ethic… no work, ever.

You will remember Slick, my Black Tomcat pal who saved my life at least once (the Horny Owl) and Hank (the tackyturn truck driver) from 'The Nine Lives…'. Those two and me, and Godenboy, age 12, (a boy genius) constituted my gang of mischiefied friends.

<u>Editors Note</u>: *Felix, for God's sake stop pumping your first book. That is pathetic.*

<u>Arthurs Note:</u> *You mean "The Nine Lives of Felix the Tomcat" by me on Amazon. The one described as a page burner,' and 'Riveting!'*

Hank and Slick brought my new shit into the house: an Apple 2021 MacBook Pro with 14" screen with 16 GB RAM and 512 GB SSD and a Canon top-end scanner/color printer. Goldenboy had advised me on my computer gear for the sunroom. V-Dome's Visa card worked great. Goldenboy would reimburse his distracted father… only if the goofball with the Nordic Blond wig noticed my $4000 Amazon charge on his Visa. If this was not Quality living… someone give me a kick in the ass.

Rosa, the manshun's sparkplug Guacamolan cook and maid, made us a great lunch of balonie sandwiches on Hoagie buns (I now ordered my balonie on Amazon). Me and Slick had the delicious luncheon meat, back bacon and cream. Hank had sandwich and a Rolling Rock brewski and me and Slick shared a Bud. They invited me to join them for the afternoon deliveries. Rosa chatted away in Spanish.

Hank, Slick and me took off for deliveries after lunch. Hank was playing Willie on the Bluetooth quadrifonified stereo system and Slick and me did some line-dancing on the passenger's seat. The Amazon van was super quiet… and peppy.

Hank said, "This is my best gig yet. I just work till she almost runs out of juice. Then I go home to snooze and plug her in to recharge. They pay me for eight hours."

We finished piling shit on porches of manshuns in Fox Chapel Hill Gated Community and headed toward Pittsburg.

Hank pulled into the parking lot in front of "Sven's Yogi Spa and More". We all went to the door with a package the size of a box of donuts. Some tired-looking, sweaty, guppy women were straggling out of the gym to their BMW-Yahs. Sven was in his office, wearing a tight baby blue body suit. When he stood up... his obvious asymmetry was... obvious, duh! Sven's giant carrot looked robust, but his swollen left testicle, last seen in the area of his belly button at Afrodite's party ('Nine Lives Chapter 29) had disappeared! As you recall, the disgruntled Tootsie Trammel, one of the Sven Sexy Seven had delivered a vicious carrottee kick to Svens groin with a size 10 $1200 Jimmy Choo shoe after he implied she 'vas fat' in her fashion show debut.

Sven said, "Zank de Lord, My new ball has arrived on ze scene. I had zee original amputated zee day after zee party. Zee pain vas over zee top."

He ripped open the package. Inside were 16 2 ¼ inch ISPiriRito Billiard balls (Fibreglass Resin...Amazon Prime $50.20).

Sven held up the burgandy-colored 7-ball and grinned, "Zis boll vill do nicely! Dr. Fred Slumkowski vill fix me up in zee morning. A little snip- snip and I will be better zan ever!'

Sven had researched testicular prostheses and realized that a new medical-grade siliconified go-nad would set him back $2000 plus labour (at least $10,000.) A human urologist could give him a maximum 1.5" diameter implanted prosthetic testicle... compared to Sven's healthy 3.5 inch right testicle. Sven's insurance didn't cover testicular replacement surgery. (vanity surgery)

Sven said to the human urologist, "That vill not verk!" So, Sven went to my ex-vet, Dr. Fred Slumkowski (see chapter 22 of "Nine Lives) to get a quote. Slumkowski specialized in neutering cats and dogs. His attempt on my gonads went poorly… for him!

"A Resin billiard ball… 2 ¼ inch diameter from zee Amazon. A quick snip-snip… and a very nice big go-nad back in ze strokum… $600 cash." Sven was pumped. He hoped to get back to his one-on-one work with the 'Sven Sexy Seven' Yogi group as soon as his junk was back in working order. Sven obviously had not read my 'Yelp' review on Dr. Slumkowski.

We drove on into outer Pittsburg, dropping off shit along the way. We wove through some back streets on the northern edge of Pittsburg and pulled up behind 'Starstuds and More' Store #57. (Chapter 10 'Nine Lives' book). V-Domes shiny red porch-911 was in the 'Boss' reserved parking spot behind the coffee shop.

Hank picked up a few big Amazon boxes and lugged them inside. V-Dome was planted behind the counter, drinking a double-expresso, lactose-free giant latte ($6.50 Starstuds) and giving Michaela (the hot Latino store manager) a back rub. Michaela towered over her boss, V- Dome, who owned 57 Outlet stores of Starstuds and More. The coffee shops extended all the way from New Jersey to Boston.

If you haven't read 'The Nine Lives of Felix the Tomcat' Velcrodome was my 'owner' (cat owner is an oxymoron) and stood 5 foot-three with heel lifts and was chubby and obnoxious. He wore a ridiculous Nordic Blond wig, sporting a mullet and a man-bun. He had a dyed blonde goatee and snowy white eyebrows. He held his hairpiece on with a wide strip of Velcro permanently glued to his bald head... (hence Velcro-Dome). He had added hoop earrings in both of his ears. V-Dome still looked like a Denarius Targaryen meets the Tiger King lovechild. He was married to the oh-so-gorgeous Afrodite and, possibly, had fathered Goldenboy and Gloomer.

Three swarthy looking gents, all wearing maroon velour sweatsuits, were sitting near the front door, at a table, smoking stogies and slugging expresso shots. If their names weren't Tony, Tony and Tony, my mom's an aardvark.

The biggest Tony... who went by 'Big Tall Tony', leered at V-Dome and said, "Hey, ya got our outdoor furniture at last, Rugman?"

V-Dome stammered, "Yes, 'Big Tall Tony'. We will set it up out front. Then you guys can drink your free caffeinated beverages wherever you want. The table and chairs are 'top of the line' from the Amazon Soprano Outdoor furniture collection."'

'Big Tall Tony', 'Skinny Horney Tony' and 'Hungry Fat Tony' all gave V- Dome a thumbs up and said, "Hey."

V-Dome asked, "When is 'Big Little Vinnie' coming down to P-Town again to see me?"

'Hungry Fat Tony' scowled and said, hoarsely, "Hey, Rughead, gimme a couple avocado, bacon and beef wraps… or 'Big Little Vinnie' might be down ta see you real soon! You know… Badda Bing… Badda Boom!" He put the tip of his index finger on his nose and pushed it to be more crooked.

"Powerful you have become. The dark side I sense in you." Yoda.

With Hank at the wheel we worked our way back home before we ran outa juice. Me and slick agreed to meet at our 'Happy Place' after dark for some Tomcat C, C and C (Carnivorous Cavorting and Coitus). Otherwise, I needed a serious nap.

Chapter 4

A Roman Christmas

"The main reason that Santa is so merry is that he knows where all the bad girls live." —George Carlin

Goldenboy set up my new laptop and printer in the sunroom when he got home. Being a computer whiz, he quickly showed me all kinds of short cuts and tricks. The new set up was astoundingly fast and the graphics were dynamite. I loved it.

He set up Speechify and put on the Morgan Freedom voice for me to use with my drumstick styluses velcroed to my front paws. For new readers, Speechify is Artificial Intelligence that takes any print or keyboard entry and converts it to speech at up to 800 words per minute… in any of 14 languages. Since I can type 300 words per minute Speechify lets me speak at least 150 words a minute (normal speech) in any language with hundreds of different voices. My four favorite voices were: Afrodite ("Rosa, get Felix some cream and tuna, will ya."), Morgan Freedom ("This is God speaking."), Gwynneth Pulcratrude ("Today we will put 15 Groop Rocks in our vaginas.") and of course, Darth Vader ("Luke, you are definitely my son.").

So, Goldenboy and me sat down to chat and plan our next few weeks before Christmas.

Goldenboy said, "Felix, Pope Benny LXXXIV is anxious to meet you. He respects your idealism of utilizing every sperm. He wants to bestow a knighthood on you."

Morgan Freedom (me… on speechify) replied in that deep, deep voice, "Now wait a second, son. Can the Pope confer knighthood? Thought that was the Queen's job."

Goldenboy nodded, "First, Felix, the Queen croaked a few weeks ago and that flake, Bonnie Prince Charlie, has taken over. Second, yes… the Pope can knight you into the Order of St. Gregory the Great. There are 3000 papal knights. You would become Sir Felix the Tomcat, and you would have to display courage, friendship, generosity, and piety."

I looked at Goldenboy and said, in Yoda's voice, via Speechify, "Courage I have, friendships I enjoy, generosity I practice and piety… Piety… let me get back to you on piety. Yes, a Papal Knight I shall be. Christmas, in Rome, we shall spend."

I switched back to Darth Vader, "the Holy See is waiting, Goldenboy! Book the death star… first class."

I asked one more question, "Do I have to be a Catholic?" (that would be a dealbreaker!)

Goldenboy chuckled, "Nope. And Pope Benny LXXXIV loves cats."

I asked, "Do I get a horse, a shield, and a sword."

Goldenboy shook his head, "Come on, Felix, stop fucking with me."

Goldenboy booked the flights online … we would fly on December 18th, once school was out, and visit Rome and the The Vatican. Slick and Hank and Gloomer would join us because both Afrodite and V-Dome had a lot of parties and functions to attend over the Holidays. Who could refuse a free trip to Europe. Slick and me would travel first class as 'Emotional Support Cats.'

V-Dome was planning to make a giant poster of Goldenboy, Gloomer, me, and the Pope to hang up in his 57 Starstuds and More Stores. The Pope's Emissary emailed Goldenboy to say, "All expenses paid" for the trip which would include a five day tour bus tour with a bunch of Cardinals around Italy. I planned to brush up my Italiano love language before the trip, "Sei Bello. Posso fare l'amore con te." ("You are beautiful. Can I make love to you?" Rosettas Stones)

If they were planning to knight me for spreading sperm, I might as well start my noble quest in Italy, the land of Love.

Before heading out to meet Slick, I whipped off a few psychiatric certificates stating that Goldenboy and Hank were in urgent need of Emotional Support Cats for their plane travel to Italy. I created a nice letterhead for Dr. Felix Ilgato Sirestringe, a Pittsburg shrink who specialized in PTSFD. The certificates were child's play. Slick and me were traveling first class on the Pope's dime!

Afrodite, the Goddess of the manshun, in all her beauty and wealth was very happy for me and Goldenboy. Unfortunately, at 38, in her prime, she had developed two tiny crows feet wrinkles at the outer corners of both eyes... in spite of her $600 per month Botox wrinkle-prevention budget. She endured a week long panic attack... with extra botox shots daily. Both her cheeks and her forehead were now paralyzed. Both blinking and swallow were all but impossible. Afrodite was constantly drooling. However, it helped her 500 calorie- a-day diet that she could not really chew or swallow. My Greek goddess suffered her wrinkles bravely.

Gloomer, now 16 years old, had blossomed from her grunge phase, like a Monarch butterfly. She cut her hair cut short, in a cute, white- blonde pixie cut and was playing the banjo amazingly well. She had suddenly got popular at high school and the guppy 16- year-old boys were swarming around her. 10 girlfriends texted her constantly. She had inherited Afrodite's stunning figure and good looks. She was blooming and she was pumped about our Italian adventure.

V-Dome remained his irritable, workaholic, obnoxious self. Goldenboy, Gloomer and Rosa tormented V-Dome constantly in Spanish. When he arrived home from work, for supper, Rosa shoved a plate of beef fajitas and beans and corn at him and said,

"Bueno evening, senor. Estupido idiota albino." ("Good evening, sir. You stubby albino prick." Rosetta's stones.)

Gloomer slapped her knee, howling with laughter and added, "Stupid!" ("Asshole! Rosetta's Stones)

Goldenboy was belly-laughing on the floor. V-Dome slugged back his glass of Rum and Coke and wolfified his supper. Afrodite was busy checking her wrinkles on her iPad camera. Her kale smoothie dribbled out of the corners of her mouth and dripped off her chin.

Slick and me had a great night on the prowl… hunting and snacking on birds and rodents. We chased a lost coon dog for miles until he finally ran outa gas… and puked. With our restored youth, Slick and me were an incredible tag team.

We headed back to the Sleep Safe Trailer Park for some frisky con-sexual coitus with 8 horney Queens who were thrilled to make our acquaintance. I tried out my new Italian love language... it worked better than French. Two of the Queens were visiting from Little Italy (Bloomfield) in Pittsburg and they talked like they were mobbed-up. Italian was the language of love.

We drove from Pittsburg to Washington Dulles to catch the overnight direct flight to Leonardo da Vinci Airport in Rome. I admired Leonardo and recently read a biography about him on Kindle. I told Slick about Leonardo... he could paint, draw, sculpt and think... all at the same time. He thought up the airplane, the parachute, the helicopter, diving equipment and a multi-barreled cannon (machine gun)... all back in 1500. He had an IQ of at least 180 (like me).

V-Dome loaned Hank a five-year-old Cadillac for the trip. Hank's F150 shit-box had died an honorable death. The Vatican gave Goldenboy a Visa card for our flights, meals, hotels and parking. The Vatican exceeded my low expectations in every way.

Rosa tried to sneak into Gloomers suitcase... but we heard her giggling in the trunk of the Caddy. The four hour trip to Dulles International was smooth. Hank (bass) and Gloomer (Banjo) and Goldenboy (tenor) sang and played along to Willie...

"On the road again

Like a band of gypsies we go down the highway

We're the best of friends

Insisting that the world keep turning our way

And our way is on the road again."

Gloomer had a natural gift for the banjo. Me and Slick were line dancing on the back seat. We wailed a Tomcat duet along with Roy Orbison on 'Crying'. Gloomer had tears in her eyes.

We got to the airport in good time and got into first class on the British Airways 777 bird. Me and Slick were warmly accepted as Emotional Support Cats (ESCs). The flight attendants served us cream in Champlain flutes. Hank and Goldenboy pretended to have PTFSD (Post Traumatic Fucking Stress Syndrome) by blinking a lot and letting out little "Whoop-whoop" noises until we took off.

"Benvenuto in Italia."

Chapter 5

Sir Felix and Pope Benny LXXXIV (84th)

"What did the Roman senator say after a lion ate his wife?" "Gladiator!" (A Felix joke.)

We were greeted at the luggage carousel by a priest in a black robe with a white clerical collar and a funny little pill-boxy black hat with a pom-pom on top. The priest held a big sign, "Sir Felix and Entourage." and grinned at me and Slick like we were choirboys. He led us out to a huge mutherfuckin Black Mercedees Van with picture windows that said, "Jesus loves you… if you are Catholick," on the sides with shiny gold letters and a picture of the Pearly gates. (which looked nothing like the real deal).

We drove into central Rome, weaving our way through the ancient city, 2800 years old on the Tiber River. Rome was incredible… everything was ancient. I have never seen so many statues and churches, all antique. The Romans drove like maniacs.

Our driver, Mario, was Formula One material… going around the traffic circle on two wheels and yelling out the window, "Vaffanculo, stronzo. Guido per il papa!" ("Fuck you, asshole. I drive for the Pope.") Mario told us that he had a serious shot with the Ferrari Team. The other drivers showed Mario zero respect. Mario's greatest fame as a driver was placing fourth in the 2019 Mille Miglia, a famous Italian antique (pre 1957) car race. Pope Benny LXXXIV backed Mario, in a restored, souped-up 1956 Popemobile.

We got dropped off in St. Peter's Square in front of the Apostolic Palace where the Pope and a whole pile of Cardinals lived. The Swiss Guardsmen were standing all around dressed really oddly: they wore old-fashion metal headgear that looked like pointy firemen's helmets, with bright red feather plumes running front to back. Most wore metal armour on the top, like Sir Lances-a lot, over a bright striped yellow, red, blue, and white outfit. They sported puffy shirts on top and Baggy pantaloons on the bottom. The Swiss Guards brandished 8-foot pointy spears with axes on the front called halberds. I had a flashback to losing a life to the Pittsburg butcher's meat cleaver. (see Ho…Chapter 3… 'Nine Lives.')

The guards were totally military: yelling orders at each other, playing snare drums and marchifying around like it was Mardi-Graw. Oddly, they kept snapping each other 3 finger salutes (thumb, forefinger and middle- finger)... a bit like Star Trek. Their only job was to protect the Pope and the Cardinals from 7 million tourists per year. A few of them in plain clothes packed pistols or machine guns, just in case.

Mario told us that being a Swiss Guard was a sweet gig: free housing, free food, free health insurance, free school for kids and no income tax. However, you had to be: Swiss, male, age 18-30, Catholick, not short (V-Dome was out), single, and ready to fight to the death for the Pope. The Guards could marry after the age of 25 if they got to be corporals.

If someone told 'the View' about this bastion of male privilege… old Whoopi would give them a whoopin'. Anyway, we got a special Swiss guard possee to lead us up to our quarters in the Apostolic Apartment complex. We ate a lunch of delicious Southern Italian fried Chickun, cream and bacon. Hank had a few Peroni brewskis. We all crashed for the afternoon (overnight flight) in small but comfy clerical apartments within the Palace. Many clergy had gone to their homes around the world for the holidays.

We planned to meet with Pope Benny LXXXIV at 6 PM at the Annual College of Cardinals Christmas dinner in the Sistine Chapel. Slick and me gave ourselves a good licking and Goldenboy and Hank wore suits and Gloomer wore a pretty crimson ball gown. At least 150 Cardinals wandered in, dressed alike in crimson vestments (choir gowns) and wearing red hats called galeros that looked like cowboy hats with tassels. The head table, featuring the Pope and me and my entourage, was positioned directly below Michaelangelo's ceiling painting of God pointing his finger at poor old Adam. The Cardinals were a rowdy crew, pounding on the tables and chanting, "Sir Felix, Sir Felix. Tell us a Joke, Tell us a Joke."

A lot of wine was being gulpifyed by the holy men. As the guest of honor, I got to sit on a mini throne on the head table next to His Holiness the Pope. Pope Benny dressed formally for the Christmas feast: He carried his tall walking stick with a cross on top (ferula) and wore a pure white choir gown topped with a heavy silver and gold vestment that ran down to his knees. He wore a tall pointy white and gold hat sideways on his head, making him look slightly like an alien.

Pope Benny said the blessing and invited the Cardinals to dig in. He sat down to chat with us. He was very nice and friendly, with a heavy German accent, like Sven. He looked me in the eye and said, "Vell, Felix, you haf been a wery busy boy vit Harvard, stand-up comedy and verld-chattering science break-trues, Yah? My thoughts on ze knighthood are zeese vones,"

He continued, "Ve should restore ze Order of the Golden Seal for you. Ze last Golden Seal knight died in 2019. Ve will rename it 'Ze Order of Ze Golden Sperm.' You will be zee first inductee, Sir Felix the Fiesty."

I was caught momentarily despeechified. Goldenboy had set up Speechify on my ipad. I quickly typed, a la Morgan Freedom.

"Hi Pope Benny LXXXIV, this is God speaking through Felix... or Felix speaking through God. Yep, Your Holiness, a Knight of the Golden Sperm sounds great. Do I get a shield and a sword and a horse?"

The Pope looked a bit pissed, "No, Sir Felix the Fiesty, you get a free Christmas dinner with the cardinals, a framed certificate of knighthood, a free holiday in Italy and five free Papal T-Shirts, signed by me. That's it. You must vow not to waste your sperm. You don't even need to be a Catholick."

He chuckled and took a huge bite of turkey with cranberry sauce and a big slug of red wine. With his mouth full he said, "I love zee cats."

There I sat in a hall of 150+ hungry cardinals and a celibate Pope talking about wasting sperm. (Geez Loueez, define Irony!)

<u>Editor's Note:</u> *Felix, you are, once again, on a slippery slope that ends in the Tiber River with a concrete block chained to your back paws.*

Arthur's Note: *Dear editor, fuck off. It's my story to tell!*

We all ate our fill of the delicious food. Slick and I stuck to turkey (now that was a bird) and cream and crispy bacon. We shared a glass of Burgundy wine in a golden chalice. Hank and Goldenboy and Gloomer chatted happily with the Pope and the young priests who were servers. It was a great festive meal.

After a dessert of Italian lemon gelato and Christmas cake, the Pope stood up and cleared his throat. He grabbed the mike and said, 'Tonight, it vill be my pleshure to induct zi Yankee Tomcat, ze Felix, as the first Papal Knight of ze brand new Papal Order of Ze Golden Sperm.'

He tapped me on both shoulders and on my bean with a breadknife. Sitting in my little throne facing the Pope, for some reason, I had developed a chubby, which the Pope noticed... so, for good measure, he knighted both my gonads with a tap on each of my boys. Someone snapped a picture at that very moment.

Pope Benny LXXXIV handed me a framed Certificate of Knighthood and a pile of Papal autographed T-shirts. He muttered in my ear, "Dos T-shirts are vorth $200 each on E-bay. Now behave yourself, Sir Felix the Fiesty. Don't vaste dos sperms!"

About 40 Cardinals stood up and began to sing (in 14-part harmony) the old Papal hit, from Monty Python,

"Every sperm is sacred.

Every sperm is great.

If a sperm is wasted,

God gets quite irate."

The Pope gave Gloomer a little nudge and she stood up and belted out, in a clear soprano voice,

"Let the heathen spill theirs,

On the dusty ground.

God shall make them pay for

Each sperm that can't be found."

Then all the Cardinals, led by the Pope, swinging his ferula staff like a drum-major, marched militantly around the room singing the last chorus in 37 part harmony.

After the show, the Cardinals all sat down and the Pope said, "Ok, Sir Felix, First Knight of ze Golden Sperm… ve need a few jokes while ve drink ze expressos."

The Cardinals were going nuts. What a crowd. Goldenboy set up Speechify and I strapped on my IPad styluses. I started with a Heaven joke:

"So, Pope Harry the Fourth died and arrived at the Pearly Gates. St. Peter welcomed him warmly and took him in

to sit with God, who was eating supper. God invited Pope Harry to join Him. The meal was a cold tuna sandwich on brown bread and water. Harry could see down to Hell. In Hell, they were having a party for newly arrived lawyers and politicians: steak, lobster, caviar, champagne… the works. Not wanting to complain, Harry relaxed for the evening in his modest motel room. Heaven was pretty dead.

The next evening, God invited Harry back to share supper Again, it was the same supper… cold tuna on brown bread and water. Harry looked down to Hell. They were celebrating Putin's birthday and Donald Rump was visiting (on sabbatical). The sinners were feasting on roast pheasant, sweet potatoes, barbequed spare ribs, twenty-two different salads, and twenty flavors of Haagen-Dazs Ice Cream.

Harry, feeling a bit disappointed in Heaven said, "God, what's up with the food. Our food sucks compared to Hell."

God shook His head and replied, "You know Harry, it just isn't worth cooking for two."

The Cardinals were rolling on the floor laughing and the Pope's hat had fallen off. Pope Benny held up a finger for one more joke:

I spoke in Morgan Freedoms voice. *"God speaking with a joke that Mary told me the last time I was in Heaven."*

The Cardinals and the Pope all laughed. I continued,

"So, the Pope died and the College of Cardinals gathered in Rome to choose a new pope. The leading candidate was WW2 flying ace called Cardinal Roger Mason who had flown Spitfires in the Battle of Britain. After shooting down 18 Messerschmidt German fighters in 30 days he crashed his Spitfire into trees in Normandy and lost his left arm at the shoulder. He returned to university after the war and became a Catholick priest. His first ministry was in a desolate African village with a silver mine. One night the silver mine caught fire, deep in the bowels of the earth. Heroically, Roger rushed in and saved 28 miners. Unfortunately, Roger was blinded in the left eye by a shard of wood when the mine collapsed around him. The burning silver also stained all his skin a bright purple color."

Felix paused.

The Pope said, "Well, Sir Felix, who was elected Pope?"

Felix replied, "Oh, a guy from Poland won. The Catholick church was not ready for a one-eyed, one-armed flying Purple Papal leader."

Me and Slick were dying for a little Tomcat action. Goldenboy, Gloomer and Hank headed off for bed. It had been a special night for all of us. Mario, our driver, took a bunch of pictures of the Pope, me, Gloomer and Goldenboy to make V-Dome's posters to hang up in all the Starstuds and More coffee shops.

Me and Slick headed outside to explore the Vatican. With 7 million visitors a year eating junk food, the Vatican was a mouse and rat smorgansburg. The little Italian buggers were fast, but we were faster. Queen-wise, the Vatican was equal to your average trailer park. Horney Italian Queens lurked all about, waiting for an injection of new jeanetic material from the US of A. Italians love cats… there are 120,000 feral cats in Rome. I whispered my Italian love language in the Queens' ears, "Sei una bellisimo regina." ("You are a beautiful Queen."Rosetta's Stones) It was 'Badda Bing, Badda Boom."

Chapter 6

When in Rome

"In Rome, the emperor sat in a special part of the Coliseum called the Caesarian Section."—George Carlin

Me and Slick had a big catch-up sleep in a comfy bed in a bed normally occupied by Cardinal Alphonse de Natilio from the Philippines. We got up at about 11 AM and wandered down to the Cardinal cafeteria where the cooks kept bowing toward me, "Sir Felix, come ti placebla tua pancetta?" (Sir Felix. How do you like your bacon?" Rosetta's Stones.)

All the Swiss Guards were snapping me three-fingered salutes. I was royalty. Me and Slick chowed on bacon, cream, and sardines… good carnivore fare. Big groups of stunned-looking tourists kept rambling through. The Vatican was making a killing on Tours… everything from 'the Vatican Museums, Sistine Chapel and St. Peters Basilica Tour' for $75.75 USD to the 'Private Vatican Museums &Sistine Chapel Tour' for $202.23 USD. The Catholic Church was worth $30 billion in May 2021. The Moreman Church was worth $100 billion in February 2021 showing clearly that tithing and organic growth (screwing a lot) pay off big time. Me and Slick headed back for a snooze to rest up for a night at the Coliseum.

We had a late supper with Hank, Goldenboy, and Gloomer who had a great day touring Rome with Mario. They had bought me and Slick little Cardinal hats, called galeros… the little red cowboy hats. We looked awesome and wore them to supper at a nice little pizza joint near the Vatican. Me and slick had ham, pepperoni, sausage, and cream.

There was a picture of me being knighted by Pope Benny spread across the front page of L'Osservatore Romano, the daily Vatican Newspaper. The headline read, "Prima Gatto nominato Cavaliere dal papa." ("First cat knighted by the Pope." Rosetta's stones.)

Below the headline story on Page One, was a picture of my junk being knighted by the Pope, complete with my chubby!

The caption read, "Sir Felix il Fiesty ottiens la sua spazzatura nominate cavaliere dal Papa." ("Sir Felix the Feisty Gets his Junk Knighted by the Pope."Rosetta's Stones)

I was famous… in a pervertified fashion. The pictures and articles had gone viral around the world.

Me and slick headed out on the town at dark. We were heading to the Coliseum, which was only 4 km from the Vatican. Slick and me walked by a hundred restaurants and outdoor cafes on the way. The Romans loved cats and kept throwing us little bits of pepperoni and sausage and applauding and saying "Signore Felix GiGi"… which was my new name, I guess (short for Sir Felix of the Golden Gonads.) I was fucking famous. Slick enjoyed the notoriety, I think.

We got to the Coliseum, which was a massive outdoor amphitheatre, (like the Astrodome with no roof) built before 100 AD. The walls (160 feet high) had partly collapsed and there were many arch-shaped holes through the walls. In it's prime it held 65,000 spectators.

The Coliseum hosted gladiatorial battles between men and their opponents: other men, lions, tigers, bears, bulls, hippos, elephants, crocodiles, panthers, and leopards. Over 20,000 fighting animals per year were imported from all over the Roman Empire which stretched from England to southern Egypt and included modern Greece, Turkey, Iran, Iraq, North Africa, France, Spain, and Portugal.

The Gladiators, who looked like NFL linebackers, were super-tough guys who fought with spears, swords, axes, and bare knuckles. Stubborn Christians were regularly fed to the lions and tigers for entertainment and became known as Vitamin C to the cynical Roman Senators (who called the shots in Rome). It was the beginning of live sports for the masses and was more exciting than baseball or Jeperdy reruns. Me and slick wandered inside to see the 300 foot by 200 foot central arena, the oval where all the fighting occurred.

We heard a Tomcat talking loudly in Cantonese (a universal cat language) in the first row of the seating area behind us.

He was the biggest, roughest looking tomcat I had ever seen. He was twice my size and looked like a leopard. He was missing most of his two ears and had a stubby three-inch tail. He was surrounded by forty or so big, mean-looking Tomcats. His gang were scruffy-looking cats missing teeth and parts of ears and tails.

The leader jock-walked up to me and Slick and said, 'Hey, you must be Sir Gi-Gi. You and Il Papa are tight, I hear."

We high-fived and I said, "Yes, I am Sir GiGi at your service." I bowed.

The huge leopard/Tomcat growled back, "Call me 'Il Duce'.

"My ancestors were leopards and my super-great, great grandfather was Benito Mussolini's cat...'Bubbles'." Il Duce was no 'Bubbles'! There were a lot of Toms in the gang of forty cats who looked much like Il Duce, so I gathered that he was not a virgin. All of them had super short tails and buck-teeth, so I suspected that a little sludge had crept into the gene pool. They also did not appear overly bright. We chatted for a while. Everyone was friendly in a vaguely hostile way.

After ten minutes or so, Il Duce, who was clearly the boss said, "OK, Sir Gi-Gi, time to have an Italian-USA Tag Team Rumble. Prove to us that you deserve to have your gonads plastered across every website and newspaper in the universe."

He pointed to a decrepid 93 year old silver cat with crutches and a cervical collar and said, "My tag-team partner is Rusty Silver who used to live with Cardinal Fred Silver before the priest went to the slammer." Rusty nodded and waved a crutch.

I looked at Slick. The rules were 'kill or be killed in 15 minutes,'... And 'stay inside the arena,' and,' no weapons except teeth and claws.'

Slick gave me a nod and I accepted the challenge. What could go wrong?

Slick and me retired to the underground catacombs to stretch and prepare for the Tag Team Rumble. We did a few push-ups to warm up. I said to Slick, "We got this, Pardner."

When we emerged from the tunnel, we could see IL Duce doing jumping jacks to warm up, in the center of the arena. The several hundred cats that lived at the Coliseum, were sitting in the stands, chanting, "Duce, Duce, Duce! Mangio lo Yankee! Mangio la Yankee!" ("Eat the Yankee!" Rosetta's stones).

If the crowd had its way, we were about to become a midnight snack for the home team.

As we stepped through the door into the arena, we heard a sharp cat-cry and old Rusty Silver dropped from the sky… down across our backs, snarling, biting, and snapping his dentures. We quickly wriggled loose from the geriatric assailant, and Slick booted him in the go-nads. Rusty, whining in agony, retired on the spot.

The battle now was reduced to two cunning Yankees versus one large, strong, mean fucking mini-leopard who was growling with rage.

Our strategy to beating Il Duce was simple… avoid fighting him by tag-teaming him… strike and run, strike and run. We would wear the sucker out. I was the first non-macho Knight in history. Slick and me ran and jumped and dodged and weaved. I would cut in front of Il Duce, and when he chased me, Slick would bite him in the tail or the ass. Then we would reverse roles. Yes, we did each lose a chunk of an ear and a few inches of tail. However, we survived 15 minutes in the ring… alive.

To our credit, I kicked sand in Il Duce's face and Slick bit him hard in the ass… twice. The match was scored 51 to 49 for Il Duce, but the judges were all Italian and part of his gang. Slick and me were named Honorary

Coliseum Cats, which was quite an honor for Yankees. We stumbled back to the Apostolic Palace, exhausted.

Chapter 7

A Tour of Rome with the Pope/Sienna

"A difference of opinion is what creates missionaries and horseracing." —Will Rogers

The Pope's popularity numbers had risen from 31% to 77% in Poles since he knighted me and my go-nads and he was not about to waste the good PR. Pope Benny had decried my Golden Gonad picture "pornografia di gatti. ("Cat pornography" Rosetta's Stones.)

My go-nad photo was now the screen saver on 500 million iPads and laptops around the world. We joined Pope Benny, Mario, a couple of Cardinals and three couple undercover Swiss Guards (wearing the yellow, blue, red and white striped pantaloons with a jacket, shirt and Papal tie… carrying Uzis). Mario was driving respectfully because the Pope was drinking his morning coffee. Hank, Goldenboy, Gloomer, me and Slick were pumped to have a tour of Rome with a local.

We hit all the historic tourist stuff… the Trevi fountain, the Spanish steps and the Parthenon. At each stop, we all hopped out and had a photo op with the Pope… had a quick look around. Slick and me drank from the Trevi Fountain… someone had pissed in it. We chased each other up and down the Spanish Steps. The Partheon, with a famous occulus (eyeball of natural light) in the domed ceiling was pretty cool… it was built as a temple to at least 12 different gods in the first century A.D. The Pope and me had a photo op on the steps… Pope Benny made sure my junk was well hidden behind his arm.

Our last stop was the famous Torre Argentina Cat Sanctuary, located in the ruins of an old Roman Temple, covering an entire city block. Over 300 feral cats called the sanctuary home and lived among the ruins. Volunteers arrived daily to feed the cats, monitor their health and arrange adoption of cats to good homes (125 per year). While the Pope was glad-handing the locals, Slick and me caught the furrmone trail of a Queen in heat and descended some steps to an underground excavation… an old basement.

I was awestruck… in the corner, preening and swishing was the most georgeous, jet-black, long-haired, eye-lash batting, svelt Queen that I had ever seen. And, she was in heat… she looked me longingly in the eye and said, in a super sexy voice,

> "Hey there, Sir Gigi, have you got your sword with you today?"
>
> I stammered, "Yes, young maiden, it is coming right up." … and, by George, it was!

We copulated like a couple of maniacs. Her name was MiMi. She had lived at the Torre Argentina for a year, carefully avoiding their neutrifying programme. We had a nice chat and I wished her well. She promised to name one of her litter GiGi after moi. I seriously considered falling in love with her… but long-distance romance is notoriously trickyfied. Besides, the word on the street was that her boyfriend was IlDuce … and I did not want to meet that fella again. Also, I like being a free Tomcat. "Live free or Die." (New Hampshire license plate.)

We headed back to the Palace for an afternoon nap. In the evening, the five of us Yankees headed out for supper and a movie, "Cinderella" (Italian with English subtitles), starring Camilia Cabello… both Goldenboy and Gloomer were in love with her. The movie, a musical, was great. We were leaving for our five-day 'Tour Italy with a Cardinal Tour' in the morning. (Tickets available Vatican Ticket Office- meals, transport and accommodation included… $1799 per person USD.)

Early in the morning, Gloomer woke us up. “Hey cats…The tour leaves at 7 AM. If you want breakfast, you better wake up.”

Me and Slick had eaten a few mice in the Sistene Chapel after the movie, so we skipped breakfast and snoozed till 6:45 Am.

We joined the Big Silver Mercedees Tour bus with 13 Cardinals in civvies, 2 Swiss Guards (undercover with striped Pantaloons and Uzis) and 18 loud, obnoxious tourists… mostly Americans with four fascist Germans and two rich Russian oligarks. What could go wrong?

Mario was driving and wheeled the 45 foot bus through the streets of Rome, heading north, like a go-cart. One of the Russians was hung-over and started to puke on two of the Germans.

The Cardinals were chanting, “Piu veloce, Piu veloce.” (“Faster, Faster”. Rosetta’s stones) Cardinals notoriously loved to fuck with tourists.

The trip up to Siena, a walled city famous for the bi-annual Palio horserace around the central Piazzo del Campo (central city square), would take us about three hours… so Slick and me had a good nap.

The bus had slowed to enter Sienna… a beautiful red brick city surrounded by walls, made up of 17 wards (neighborhoods) in constant competition with each other. Each ward had a flag, a band, a few good horses and a lot of young men filled with testosterone.

We pulled up to the Grand Hotel Continental Siena- Starhotels Collezione, which was near the Piazzo Campo square. It was pretty Swanky. Feral cats wandered around the city… much like Rome. We moved our gear up to our rooms, which were gorgeous, with big canopied king beds with spacious windows overlooking the square. Me and Slick and Hank shared a room.

We met with the whole group for lunch in the restaurant… what a spread. Me and Slick had our usual…cream, bacon and tuna served on a silver chaffing dish. The Germans scarfified beer and the Russians were doing vodka shots with the Yankees. The Cardinals seemed to be delighted to be free of Rome and chatted excitedly among themselves. Today was the Celebration of the Lost Magi… the three Wise men who took a right in Constantinople and followed the wrong star to Sienna instead of Jerusalem.

The Siennese folks celebrated the Lost Magi by having a horse race contest between the wards in the Piazza Campo followed by something called 'The Alley Chase.'

As we finished desert… lemon gelato… we heard the festivities starting up in the city square. We headed outside to watch. Led by drums and coloured flags, groups of about 100 people wearing the same colours as their flags (red and white, yellow and black etc.) Seventeen crews showed up from the 17 wards of the city. Each crew entered the Piazza from a different direction. At the back of each group walked a big horse and a rider dressed up in team colours. Leading each Horse was a skinny athletic Italian guy dressed up like Santa. Each Santa carried a big shoulder bag full of wrapped lollipops in team colours which he tosed to children and hot young women. There was a crapcaphonie of sound and colour and excitement.

The horserace would be around the edge of the square 3 times with the finish line in front of a mini-bleacher setup at the end of the longest straight-away. All the Santas and all the feral cats in town sat in the mini-bleachers to watch the race.

I had been recognized as Sir GiGi… so all the cats and Santas wanted to sit beside me for the race. A bugler got up and played a tune, then someone fired an old musket and the 17 horses and riders took off, thundering around the track. The crowd of at least 5000 Italians went crazy, everyone waving flags with their team colours. The horses raced round and round the Piazzo, slipping and sliding on the cobbled brick track. Finally, they took the last turn, 5 horses neck and neck, thundering toward us in the mini-bleacher which was six feet high.

As the horses crossed the finish line, Me and Slick realized that we were alone in the mini-bleachers. I turned around… all the feral cats and Santas were running down the alley behind the bleachers. I figured out what 'the Alley Chase' meant and me and Slick high-tailified our way outa the bleachers and down the Alley, ominously called 'Santa Gatto' Alley.

The 17 horses leaped over the bleachers and pounded their way down the alley behind us. Now, me and Slicked weren't the two fastest cats in the world... but we passed a lot of Santas and a lot of feral cats in the next few minutes. I had a horse stomp on my whiskers at one point and Slick lost another two inches of his nice new black tail. Finally, about a thousand yards into the race we saw a tall power pole and scampered up to safety. Our hearts took five minutes to stop pounding.

I said, "Slick, comrade, I am afraid that cost us a life."

Slick nodded and said, "Yup."

Vowing to be more careful... Slick and me, with 6 lives left each, headed back to the hotel for a snooze.

Chapter 8

The Cardinals and the Meaning of Life

"Please don't worry so much. In the end, none of us has very long on Earth. Life is fleeting." —Robin Williams

The hotel arranged a special dinner for us. They were honored to have 13 Cardinals and me visiting from Rome. They arranged for three regional chefs to cook their special dishes for us. Dressed in red robes and little red cowboy hats (galeros), the Cardinals looked sharp. They had been into the Chianti bigly and were very chatty. Me and slick, also wearing our red galeros, joined the party and shared a Peroni beer in a silver goblet. Hank was slugging back Peronis and Goldenboy and Gloomer were into the bubbly.

Goldenboy showed me Speechify 2.0, the newest AI software program, allowing you to talk into the mike in one language and voice…and have it instantly converted to any of 18 languages with 100 different voices. It was amazing… Each time Goldenboy (as Morgan Freedom) said, "I am God, listen up"…he translated it to a different language Even the Cardinal from Outer East Mongolia heard God speak directly to him in distinct East Mongolian. With two ipads with Speechify 2.0… anyone could talk to anyone… anywhere with complete clarity. Goldenboy had re-discovered the Tower of Babel.

We had a wonderful meal: Spaghetti alla Carbonera, Napoletana Pizza, risotto, steak Florentina, Polenta, Lasagna and Gelato.

After supper, the wait staff cleared the tables and we all clustered around two big tables to talk and drink coffee. All of the cardinals, who seemed to hang out with a special best friend, were keen to talk with ordinary Americans via Speechify 2.0. The Russians and Germans and other Americans took off to check out the nightlife in the area. I quickly realized that the Cardinals were smart, educated guys with at least a Phd or two. One of them, Cardinal Smithers, was very funny and outgoing… flamboyant would describe him.

He had a background in Vatican Stand-up… he grabbed the mike to my IPad and spoke in rapid Italian… Goldenboy's iPad translated it to English with George W. Bush's voice,

"A beloved Pope died and went to heaven." St. Peter told him, "Pope, you, being a Greek and Hebrew scholar, may have access to any of our sacred records between God and the various prophets of old."

The Pope said, "I would love to look at the translations of the instructions God gave Peter for founding the Holy Church."

The Pope spent two years in hard study, then suddenly disturbed Heaven with yelling and shouting and screams of anguish.

God walked over and said, "What is up Pope?"The Pope pointed over and over again to a single word of the ancient parchment in front of him, "There's an 'R', There's an 'R'. There's an 'R'... It's CELIBRATE, not Celibate!"

Goldenboy took the mike and spoke into speechify 2.0 in English. Morgan freedom's voice, in Italian boomed,

"Do you believe in the celibacy of the clergy?"

Father Smithers, the flamboyant Cardinal from New Orleans, imitating Bill Clinton, answered," I never had sex with that woman."

The cardinals were belly laughing.

Goldenboy followed up, "Are many priests and cardinals gay?"

Father Smithers shimmied around a bit, "You bet your ass, brother."

The other Cardinals all nodded in agreement. It became clear that we were looking at 5 'best-buddy' Cardinal pairs and, possibly, a three- way... a throuple. The two Swiss Guards were holding hands in the corner... their Uzis at the ready.

I asked, via Typing into Speechify, "So Cardinal, is it easier to be a priest if you are gay...?"

The thirteen cardinals all nodded in unison. One of the more serious Cardinals asked Goldenboy, "What do you Believe in, son? Is there a God?"

Goldenboy thought for a while, and answered, "Possibly there is an intelligence and a presence in the Universe much greater than us."

The Cardinals were nodding. The cardinal from Honduras, Father da Silva, a really nice fellow, said, "God is a human-made construct that we create in our minds that helps us deal with fear and death. What we need to seek is freedom from constricting ideas that prevent us from feeling peace, from communing honestly with the intelligence of the cosmos."

Gloomer asked, "Father, how do we achieve that freedom?"

Father Da silva replied, "You cast aside the cliches and the dogma and the false values of pride and materialism and power and you look inside yourself. God is inside you. Find peace and just live, now."

I asked again, "And why are priests celibate?"

The Cardinals all looked back and Father Dinardo from Madrid said, "Who the Hell is keeping score?"

The priests all shrugged their shoulders.

And I asked, "Is my sperm really precious?"

Cardinal Dinardo replied, "To whom?"

And the priests chuckled, then they all shrugged again.

Gloomer asked, "So is there a Heaven and Hell?"

Father Smithers swooshed around a bit and replied, "Heaven and Hell are right here on earth, sister! We construct them."

I asked, "How about Buddists, Muslims, Shintus, Hindus, Moremans, JWyahs and all the other believers… who is right and who is wrong?"

Cardinal Dinardo replied, "They all believe different human constructs about their existence on Earth that makes them feel better. All human constructs are mere illusions. Religions are illusions shared by groups of people. Reality is much more simple and it lives quietly inside us until we make the effort to discover it."

It was a wonderful, enlightened discussion that I truly enjoyed. I developed a new deep respect for the Cardinals, especially Cardinal Dinardo.

Chapter 9

How 'I (almost) Lost my Gonads in San Gimignano'

"If it has tires or testacles it is going to give you trouble."
—Anon

If that title was not a Sinatra tune, my mother was a walrus and my father was an albacore tuna! We order room service for breakfast... fabulous bacon, cream, sausage...hey, I am an obligatified carnivore.

Cardinal Dinardo invited Me, Goldenboy and Gloomer to tour the stunning Sienna Cathedral with him and Cardinal Ferreira, from Portugal, who was his long-term partner. Cardinal Dinardo had been Professor of European Studies at Loyola University in Chicago before becoming a Cardinal. Cardinal Ferreira's background included professorships in Biology and Genetics at the University of Lisbon and at the Sorbonne in Paris.

Sienna cathedral was 5 blocks from the hotel, so we walked over with the Cardinals, stopping for expresso along the way. Goldenboy set me up with Speechify so that I could chat with the holy men while sipping my saucer of cream. I had little use for caffeine... it made me jumpy and ruined my napping.

Gloomer and Goldenboy were seriously into expresso with lots of sugar. We chatted about architecture... the Duomo (cathedral) di Sienna was built of Tuscan marble around 1300AD and featured arches, columns, gargoyles, saints, steeples and 3 massive arched entry portals. It was called Tuscan Romanesque in style and covered an entire city block. Father Dinardo gave a brief dissertation on how Sienna's Duomo contrasted with St. Peter's Basilica, in Rome, a Renassance Catholic shrine designed by Michaelangelo and pals. Workers needed over a hundred years to complete the massive Rome church before 1615 A.D.. St. Peter's was a huge Dome structure with an entry through five huge doors placed between six massive carved stone Roman columns. St. Peters could hold 60000 worshippers (standing) and held the bones of old St.Peter (the Rock) himself. Italy was living history.

We wandered through the Duomo, viewing the fresco paintings, the stained glass and the sculptures. The head priest buttonholed Fathers Dinardo and Ferreira to invite us to join him for expresso in his study. I sat in a little velvet armchair opposite father Rosetti, the head honcho at the Duomo, who was fingering a very sharp looking letter opener. We chatted about Papal politics and church attendance and the Church retirement plan… but he kept glancing at my junk. Finally Father Rosetti identified the elephant in the room… He stuttered a bit, in English, "And so, Sir Gi..Gi…Gi.. GiGi, to what catholic church have you pledged your go-nads when you die?" Talk about getting to the point!

"Your p-p-p-p-preciouses are now recognized as famous and precious Catholic rre…rel…rel…reli… ah,…icons. Here, at the S-S-S-Sienna Duomo we already possess half of St. Peter's ancient foreskin… we would love to add the Gonads of the First knight of the Golden Sperm to our historic display of Catholic relics. A contribution of 100,000 Euros could be forwarded to your estate today, payable in Bitcoin."

My God, if V-Dome or Afrodite ever heard about this… I would be sold…instantly… for parts! I quickly ske-daddled outa there…

Editor's Note: Felix, you asshole, has it occurred to you that you have written more than 5000 words about nothing except your go-nads and the perilous state of their existence. Get a life, moron.

Arthur's Note: Easy for you to say, Editor. A) Your go-nads are not on the cutting board here. B) You haven't got every thug in Europe vying to snatch your go-nads for cash.

After a nice snooze and lunch, the entire group took off in the Papal coach to experience some of the beautiful hill country between Sienna and Florence. It was spectacular terrain... grainfields, olive groves and vineyards with ancient stone farmhouses. All the little towns were built around 1300 A.D. on the top of high hills with walls surrounding them to repel mauraudfying armies from the competing city states...Florence, Rome, Milan, Naples and Venice.

The independent city states, called dutchies behaved much like the Mafia... controlling travel, trade, commodities, banking and political clout. All the rich families built towers as high as 150 feet to show off, but also to live in and to hide in when their town was invaded by a hostile army. Many towers had bells at the top to warn the citizens of raids.

We visited San Gimignano, an ancient town which was perched on top of a ginormous hill and was completely surrounded with 20 foot walls. It had 72 tower-houses plus 6 tall bell towers and a smallish Duomo and a Torture Museum. During the Spanish Inquisition from 1478 to 1834 the Catholick Church, especially in Spain, pursued, tortured, drownified or burned folks who they believed were learning toward either the Jewish or the Muslim religion.

Confessions of witchcraft, heresy or bigamy were forced out of suspects with torture devices such as the rack (cruel stretching bed) the iron maiden (like a mummy container with inward spikes piercing the victim), thumbscrews and the fore-runner of waterboarding. The ultimate penalty for witches was being burned at the stake (30,000+ 'witches' burned during the 350 year inquisition in Europe.

There was also widespread persecution of Jews and Muslims, including forced conversion to Catholicism. The Museum of Torture had collected torture tools from all around Europe... but, ironically, the museum had a pleasant, 'Hey, let's just be friends!' vibe.

We visited the parish priest in the mini-Duomo. After 20 minutes of small talk, the priest bid $20,000 Euro for my gonads when I die... I told him, via Speechify, in Italian, "Nei tuo sogni, Buster!" ("In your dreams, Buster!" Rosetta's Stones.)

We went for a bite of pizza and some vino in the central square and then climbed back on the coach to return to Sienna for the night.

We all had a siesta... then another wonderful meal of Italian food... The Roman's invented good dining. Then we had a multicultural talent show...

Goldenboy was the Master of Ceremonies via Speechify, as Darth Vader in Italian, Arnold Swartzenager in German and George W. Bush in Russian. First, he introduced the animated Cardinal Smithers from New Orleans who did amazing impressions of:

John Wayne; "Whoa, take her easy there, Pilgrim."

Bruce Willis, "Yippie-Kai-Yay, Motherfucker!"

Marlon Brando, "I'm gonna make him an offer he can't refuse."

Clint Eastwood, "Go ahead, make my day."

Sean Connery, "Bond, James Bond."

Arnold Schwarzenagger, "I'll be back!"

Then the Cardinal pulled out a few long female wigs...blonde and black.

He started with the dark wig:

Judy Garland, "Toto, I have a feeling we are not in Kansas anymore."

She sang "Somewhere over the Rainbow" in a clear falsetto soprano voice.

Slick and me did the Munchkin dance on the table. Then Cardinal Smithers flipped on the blonde wig, batted his eyelashes and did a great rendition of Madonna's "Like a Virgin."

He also did Elvis' "Are You Lonesome Tonight." With a mean acoustic guitar solo and a bejewelified cape and Elvis wig. The crowd, who were all guzzling beer, went wild. Fathers Dinardo and Ferreira were passing around a hookah (not a hooker) with some potent flavoured tobacco that had the pungent stink of weed.

The next act was Gloomer on Banjo and Father Belinka from Krakow, Poland on guitar playing "Dueling Banjoes" from the movie 'Deliverance'. They were amazing. Gloomer pretended to spit chewing tobacco into a cup every few minutes and Father Belinka took his dentures out for that toothless look.

At the crowds request, I gave them 10 minutes of stand-up including my favorite joke which Geoge W. Bush told in Italian:

"Gorgeous George, the iconic American Wrestling star had to battle Vivachi Vesuvio, the Italian Tornado, for the World Wide Wrestling title in Rome."

Gorgeous George's trainer reminded his fighter… "be patient and get him in your famous George sleeper hold and you should win… but do not…do NOT let him get you in the infamous Spaghetti Hold…or you are finished."

The two were an even match and grunted and grappled and threw each other about for twenty minutes. Suddenly, the crowd gasped… Vesuvio had Georgeous George in the Spaghetti Hold and it looked like the Yankee was almost done.

Suddenly the Yank exploded off the mat and knocked Vesuvio onto his back… George lept on top of the Italian and pinned him for the count of three. The Yankee was victorious.

The colour commentator asked the beaming blonde wrestler, "What happened out there, Gorgious? It looked like you were finished!"

Georgeous George grinned modestly, "Well, I was all tied up in the Spaghetti Hold. My arms were tied in reef knots and my legs were tied together in a bowline. I was on my back. When I looked up I saw a pair of testicles dangling in front of my nose... so I bit them... You cannot imagine the surge of power that shoots through a man when he bites his own balls!"

Gloomer (banjo) and father Belinka (acoustic guitar) led us in some beautiful Christmas carols... many of the Cardinals had lovely voices and were dying to sing solos. The Swiss Guards did some serious yodelling and Slick and Goldenboy sang "On the Road again," with me and Slick line dancing on the table and Gloomer on the banjo.

Chapter 10

'Oceans 27-Christmas in Venice'

"Feline just fine in Venice."—Felix the Tomcat

We were on the Papal Coach with Mario at the wheel by 9:30 AM. Everyone was hung-over except the two Russians… who had disappeared and were likely hung-over somewhere else. Mario let Interpol and the Italian cops know… those two oligarks always carried a wad of 500 Euro bills rolled up in their pants pockets. So, do the math.

Editors Note: *Can't you spell 'kidnapped', Felix?*

Arthur's Note: *Suffocate yourself, Editor.*

The trip up to Venice took us through the rolling hills of Tuscany up to the walled city of Arezzo where we stopped for expresso and pastries and gelato (yum). Slick and me had cream and balogni... a pork sausage from Bologna, Italy. I was developing cowsmopolitan tastes with my travels.

Mario took us through the countryside over to the Adriatic Sea, which was a stunning Cerulean blue-green. The Adriatic separated Italy from the Balkans (Albania, Bosnia, Herzigovinia, Croatia ... yada, yada.)

We stopped for lunch in the town square of Commanchio, a town built on the salt marshes beside the River Po right around 27 BC. It was like a mini-Venice with canals and bridges and only 22000 people. The city flourished in the salt trade and was famous for eels caught in the wetlands. After lunch (eels...slimy) we headed up to Venice, 2 hours by Mario express. To get to Venice, which was 2 ½ miles out in the Bay of Venice, we crossed a long bridge called the Ponte della Liberta.

The city itself seemed to be flooded... water everywhere. All the tourists (mostly Asian) were riding around in boats in the canals that invaded the ancient city which was built on 118 islands, with 400 bridges in about 800 AD. Whoever planned that city got an F- in the urban planning course at University of Milan. The boats in the canals were tippy...long and skinny and powered by gondoliers in black and white tops and little flat straw cowboy hats. The gondoliers pushed their boats along with poles (shallow water) and were singing their hearts out. The boats were called gondolas.

We checked into a really great hotel called the Palazzo Veneziano-Venice Collection which was central and pretty swank. I was immediately recognized as the now-famous Sir GiGi... my photos (wink, wink, Editor) had gone viral. The Pope's popularity among Poles had skyrocketed to 99.4% (second to Polish garlic smoked pork sausage which remained at 99.9%). Slick and me had a serious nap in preparation for an evening gondola tour of Venice and a banquet with the Cardinal and bishops and priests of the city. The two Russian Oligarks wandered into the hotel dining room during lunch...they were buck naked and both were missing their heavy gold chains, Rolex watches, gold bracelets and gold teeth. They looked beaten.

The boat tour of Venice was really cool. The canals wander all through the city and our gondolier could sing... ours was a lively, twenty-year-old woman from Venice who sang everything from Adele ('Hello', 'Skyfall', and 'Make You feel my Love') to Taylor Swift ('Shake it Off' and 'I Knew You were Trouble') plus the usual 'Old Solo Mio' stuff.

Goldenboy and Gloomer took me with them in one gondola and Slick jumped in with Hank and Mario. As we passed the rotting, waterlogged foundations of the buildings I saw thousands of mice and rats and hundreds of feral cats hanging out. The whole city looked ready to collapse into the Bay of Venice. Venice was sinking.

Venice had banned big cruise ships (up to 1200 feet long) from coming into the deep canals to dock in Venice in 2019. Groups of environmentally-conscious citizens felt that the big ships pollutified the water (it was plenty skanky!) and shookified the foundations of the buildings near the cruise ship docks. Venice's toilets dump directly into the canals.

We passed the biggest cruise ship docked near the city… it was only 25,000 tons and only 160 metres long (500 feet)… and had been parked in Venice Harbour for 3 years. The Vatican bought it really cheap (Benny was all business) after the ship set the world-wide record for Covid cases and deaths on cruise ships in 2019. The cruise ship was refurbished and renamed "The Corona." The Vatican advertised and sold "Corona Cruises" in Catholick papers, websites and gift-shops all around the world.

"Boost your immunity to Covid. Spend the first relaxing week exploring the history, the foods, the sights, the smells and the sounds of Venice in a four star canal-side hotel. Then join us on "the Corona". We guarantee that you will catch Covid-19 (97% success rate), and that you will not die (98.5 % success rate) and that you will have a great antibody response (92% success rate) and you will have a fabulous week dining, dancing and relaxing aboard the "Corona" while quarantined in the fabulous "City of Canals." Daily covid testing and prophylactic "Paxlovid" (a wonderful new drug treatment for Covid) provided daily at no extra charge. No one has ever got seasick on "the Corona cruise"(100 % success)."

"Passengers who are Covid positive on arrival get a 40% discount. Long Covid sufferers welcome. The two week 'cruise' from 'Venice to Venice'... basic double occupancy (city view) is $5200 USD per person." There were the usual glowing testimonials. ("It was kinda fun in spite of the chlamydia.")"

After the canal tour, Slick and me, who were getting a bit tired of the company: the balding, chubby, gay, geriatric, Cardinal crowd. We decided to have a nap and then have a tomcat-only adventure . We planned some serious mousing, ratting and Queening... if at all possible.

Gloomer and Goldenboy took off for a karaoke bar-hopping tour with Hank and Mario, along with the Yankees and the Germans. In Italy, anyone could drink alcohol, if you were breathing... but you could not buy it till you were 18 years old. The Russians had gone into hiding and had developed a paranoids.

Slick and me headed outside about 8 PM. There were mice and rats everywhere. Italian rodents are big and nasty and have no love for cats. We met three packs of at least fifteen rats... there was tons of garbage. We worked together tag-teaming lone rats or mice mostly... the mice were crunchy and wiggled nicely on the way down the hatch. The rats tasted a little off… all the sewer water, I guess. We ran into 6 smokin'hot, horney Italian Queens and managed to inject some Yannkee Tomcat sperm into them. I don't think any of the Italian Tomcats, who were plenty big and mean, were literate… none of them recognized me as the First Knight of the Papal Order of the Golden Sperm. They all called me and Slick, "Stronzi Yankees." (Yankee assholes." Rosetta's Stones.)

About 10:00 PM we noticed a lot of bright lights and commotion and a helicopter hovering over the Grand Canal…the wide, deeper waterway that ran west to east through the heart of Venice. We wandered over to a big dock, water-taxi stand extending into the Grand Canal. A movie was being filmed.

A loud American director, Steven Stonenburger, was yelling, "Oceans 27- Christmas in Venice" is going to be the best fucking movie of 2023. Look at the fucking cast, will ya!"

In front of the dock in a torpedoed-shaped bright red 40 foot speed boat sat Tom Cruiser (driving), Arnold Schwarzeneggen, the Rock (shotgun) and Bruce Willies… obviously the four action heroes of the movie.

In six other multi-coloured 30 foot speedboats nearby (bumping into each other) sat 23 more Hollywood stars… Julie Roberta, George Cloobey, Brad Pitter (staring handsomely into the middle distance), Matt Diamond, Andy Garcita, Meryl Strep, the four Balwig Brothers, Bernie Mac, Denzel W., Mr. Bean, the ubiquitous John Goodyman, Cher, Sonny, Bono, Cardi B., Jame Corbone (who is in every movie made in 2022… even Cinderella) and yada, yada… you get it.

Anyway, the obnoxious director was yelling through the megaphone… "OK, gang… the 77 evil Somali Pirates… have seized the Christian Outreach Cruise Ship."

He pointed to a massive plywood structure 1200 feet long and 12 stories high with funnels on top built to resembling a big fake mother of a cruise ship located on the other side of the canal.

"The heroes," he added, pointing to Tom, Arnold, Bruce and 'The Rock', "will race around the entire island three times, pursued by Somali terrorists in speedboats with live ammo."

He pointed up… "The helicopter will illuminate and film the boat race. After three laps the heroes will crash their speed boat into the cruise ship at 100 miles an hour. The ship will explode and the 77 evil Somali Pirates will die."

He waved his arms at the other 23 star actors in speed boats. "Then the extas… the 'extra stars'… will race across the canal and recapture the Christian Cruise ship. You will heroically recapture the ships deck and set up 2000 Christmas trees with lights."

"Then, the entire cast will then sing "Away in the Manger" with Bono on guitar."

Meryl Strep, who was now standing on the dock in an 'Abba' outfit said, "Extras…extras! Fuck this!"and walked off the set.

The other 'extra stars' were too far out in the water to join her. The scene started and the four action stars took off down the canal at 80 miles per hour with the helicopter filming them with bright lights shining down on them. (The 'Rock', Tom, Bruce and Arnold insisted on doing their own stunts.)

The 77 real Somali Pirates, who had figured out that the cruise ship was a plywood fake, all jumped into 20 dark black, villainous-looking speed boats gave chase to the four action stars, firing machine guns willy-nilly with live ammo. No bonafide Somali Pirate can resist a speedboat race or live ammo.

All the other 22 'Star Extra' actors in speed-boats gunned their engines and took off after the action stars and the Somali Pirates and the camera … hoping for some screen action shot minutes. No actor can resist a camera.

The 77 pirates had come to Venice primarily to steal St. Mark's original bones (Sacred Catholic Relics) from the gargantuan St. Mark's Basilica. This was a church so massive and heavy (built 1100s) that it was causing Venice to sink. The pirates planned to ransome St. Mark's genuine bones back to the Vatican for enough cash to build a seaside resort-motel with tennis courts and a swimming pool on the Somali coast of the Indian Ocean.

The resort would serve as a home base from which they could launchify their pirate missions in reasonable comfort.

Most of the Somali pirates had ADHD. Unfortunately, when they saw the massive cruise ship (fake) just sitting there in Venice… they hit the sucker hard. (They craved nefarious action.)

Then the boat races (with live ammo) started up… No decent pirate could restify in a deck chair.

The dock behind me and Slick was packed with interested tourists… mostly Asian. The bright red 'action-star' speedboat roared by the dock after circuit number one followed by 20 black pirate speed boats (with live ammo) and 6 Extra-star speedboats. (shooting blanks)

They had taken Alex Baldwig's gun away, but his three brothers were smokin'. The plan was to complete 3 full circles through the canals in Venice, then crash into the fake Cruise Boat to blow it up and kill the pirates.

However, the pirates had migrated to speedboats… chasing the action stars. Fortunately, or not, a painter on the fake yacht lit his cigar beside a big can of gasoline… and the huge fake cruise boat was already on fire.

Slick and me could hear the roar of the speed boats and the following machine gun fire approaching our dock again after the third trip around Venice. The red boat (action heroes) was approaching mighty fast and close to the dock.

Geraldo, who was the movie colour-commentator on the dock, dropped his voice to a dramatic whisper, "Folks, the action stars in the red boat look like they are going to hit the fucking dock!"

And then he jumped in the water. His dark wig floated free of his bald scalp.

Suddenly, me and Slick were lifted by our neck fur and tossed into the heroes' speed boat as it swept by, going 100 mph toward the fake cruise ship. I looked back... there was Ho, that treacherous Pittsburg butcher (Nine Lives), shaking his fist, and yelling,

"Got ya, Suckers!"

We crossed the canal in seconds... Arnold yelled, "I'll be back!"

And all six of us jumped overboard just before our speed boat crashed into the wooden cruise ship mock-up.

The whole damn fake ship exploded in flames shooting hundreds of feet into the air. Cats, especially Bengal cats, can swim. However, Slick and me quickly jumped on to the heads of our action star swimmers... I chose Tom Cruiser' who had serious hair. Slick had to dig in his claws to get a grip on 'the Rock's' bean. With all his muscles, Rock swam like a brick. By the time we reached the shore all the Somali pirates (77), and all the extra stars (22) had gathered on the 'fake deck' of the cruise ship. 2000 Christmas trees (10-20 feet tall) lit up the deck and the 22 extras (minus Meryl Strep) were in the third chorus of "Silent Night." The Somali pirates with ADHD fired their AK-47's into the crisp night air.

Slick and me agreed that a loss of half-a-life was appropriate for that little brush with death. (down to 5 ½ lives each) The final scene of the movie showed the 26 actors and 77 pirates sharing eggnog with the blazing fake cruise ship illuminating the night.

Slick and me did some line-dancing to "We wish You a Merry Christmas", but that scene got cut from the movie for a two-minute lingering shot of Brad Pitter looking bravely into the middle distance. 'Oceans 27-Christmas in Venice' was the #1 Christmas movie in 2023. The 'Rock' was nominated for an Oscar for, 'Best action star fighting Somali Pirates.' Slick and me got an honorable mention for 'Best Line-Dancing by Cats Cut from a Major Motion Picture.'

Chapter 11

Florence and The Leaning Tower of Pisa

"I saw the angel in the marble and carved until I set him free."—Michaelangelo

The Papal Tour Bus, Mario at the helm, took off for Florence at 9 AM. The drive through the lovely Etruscan countryside was stunning and we arrived at the city of Bologna, on the plain created by the river Po at the foot of the Appennine Mountains. The home of the oldest university in Europe (1088 A.D.), Bologna featured Spanish-style red tile roofs on its buildings. We stopped in the ancient city square for expresso, pastries and, of course, a big bowl of balogni for me and Slick.

Me and Slick discussed the fact that our life totals had dropped from 7 to 5 ½ in one month since we were last 'dead-dead' in Heaven with Budda. We needed to reform or we would be 'dead-dead' again by summer. We adopted a careful 'Life-conservifying strategy': avoid boats and action heroes, avoid cats that look like leopards, and avoid that maniac butcher from Pittsburg… Ho!

In Florence, in the Piazzale-Michaelangelo, Mario stopped the coach for us to view the 17 foot bronze replica of David…holding his sling and bag of stones to bravely fight Goliath. David also had ADHD.

We arrived in Florence for lunch and , once again, had a swanky hotel in central Florence, near the huge Duoma cathedral, the central market, the Uffizi Gallery, the Ponte Vecchio (interesting covered bridge) and the fabulous Renaissance art by Michaelangelo and his gang.

After lunch, Mario sidled up to me and Slick and Hank, Gloomer and Goldenboy and said: "Do you folks want to rent a 'Porshe" on the Pope's dime and whip over to Pisa to see the Tower?"

We were keen to go. Mario showed up in a sleek black Porshe Cayenne SUV. We jumped into the car and sped west on the super- highway A12 toward Pisa. There was a howling west wind at 100 km/h blowing in off the Ligurian Sea (part of the Mediterranean). The speed limit was 130 km/hour…but Mario handled the black beast comfortably at 160 km/hour. A cop chased us for a while… but Mario lost him.

We got to Pisa, on the Mediterranean, in the middle of a cyclone. The leaning tower, built around 1200 A.D., was built on soft ground, and started leaning immediately. The tower is 185 feet (56m) tall. The tilt got up to 5.5 degrees in 1990… and the base was partially repaired. If, by earthquake or wind, the tilt got to be over 5.5 degrees, engineers projected it would come tumbling down.

We walked around the tower and noticed a huge busloads of Asians, including Ho from Pittsburg, unloading to climb the tower in the hurricane. Geraldo, who worked for the Italian Weather Channel was doing a documentary, "La Torre di Pisa Crollera Oggi?" (Will the Tower of Pisa Blow over Today? Rosetta's Stones).

I figured, between the drenching rain, the howling wind, and Ho and 200 of his friends and relatives waving from the tiltified top of the Tower, today might be the day.

Giraldo braced himself against the wind on the 'leaning 'side of the Tower. The Tower appeared to be swaying in the howling gale. Could today be the day the famous tower toppled?

Unfortunately, we were driving at 110 km/hr through downtown Pisa when we heard the crash. Somehow, we missed the entire spectacle. Slick and me high-fived… no cat lives lost. I hoped that Ho had met his maker. Karma sucks, Sucker!

Back in Florence, Slick and me had some cream and bacon, then a nap to prepare for a night on the town in Florence. We attended a final supper feast with the entire traveling group… we had got to enjoy all the travelers… especially father Dinardo, who was smart and funny.

The Russians emerged from hiding to hit all the gold shops on the Ponto Vecchio. The supper was excellent. We sang Christmas carols and Father Smithers gave us all his best impressions again, including Somali pirates racing motor boats against Arnold, Bruce, Tom and the Rock. He even did Meryl Strep stomping off the movie set and Geraldo jumping into the polluted Grand Canal of Venice.

After dark, Me and Slick headed down to the huge Mercato Centrale (Central Market) nearby for some serious pursuit of mice, rats and Queens… We struck it rich and had a great time doing what comes naturally to a healthy, horny Tomcat.

In the morning, we headed back to Rome. Pope Benny wanted an audience with us before we headed back to the US. His popularity had soared among Poles and His Holiness was now ahead of Polish garlic sausage and bratwurst among Poles. We had a luncheon with Pope Benny and Cardinal Dinardo at 1 PM.

The Pope wanted to re-enact my knighting ceremony with a proper sword and better lighting to be made into a PR movie for the Vatican So, instead of a butter knife the Pope, who I think had mild Parkinsonism, was waving this 3 foot sword around my Golden Go-nads in what I felt was a shaky fashion.

At the end of the visit, Benny looked me in the eye and said, "Vell, Sir Felix, Dis wisit has been great. You are an outshtanding feline. Vould you consider leavink your go-nads to the Watican archives the next time you are dead-dead? Ve may be able to arrange ze sainthood of Sir Felix, if you can do ze miracle."

I figured it was miracle enough that I still had my go-nads. I told Benny that my Pittsburg agent and lawyer would get back to him on the go-nad issue.

Editor's Note: Felix, there you are back on your go-nads again. Get a life already.

Arthur's Note: Oh yes, editor, when was the last time you had a shaky 3 foot sword pressed into your junk? Gheesh!

Mario got us to the Airport in record time and we embarkified on our return journey to the USA.

Chapter 12

Pittsburg Home: V-Dome gets Connected

"Just when I thought I was out... they pull me back in." —Michael Corleone

When we walked back into the manshun, Afrodite and V-Dome greeted us with enthusiasm. We showed V-Dome the blowed-up photo portrait of Goldenboy, the Pope, Gloomer, Slick, and me... the Pope was hanging on to his shaky 3 foot sword and wearing his funny white hat sideways. Goldenboy ordered sixty-five 3 foot by 4 foot posters to hang in all the Starstuds and More coffee shops along the East Coast.

Afrodite had eradicated her two little crowsfeet wrinkles and looked as elegant and stunning as usual. Rosa made us a delicious supper of fajitas, corn, beans and rice. The family actually had a conversation with no ipads or phones. Some eye contact was made. V-Dome invited the teens to come down to visit a bunch of coffee shops with him to meet the staff and hang the posters. Of course, I was the guest of honor. I planned to wear my little silver cape (from my flying days…'Nine Lives') and my red Cardinal hat.

We were all tired… but we opened some Christmas gifts and sang a few Christmas carols with Gloomer on the banjo. My best gift was a new psychedelic neck scarf from Goldenboy. It would probably add to my allure when Queening with Slick. Slick and me had agreed to take a night off prowling and hunting to celebrate Christmas with family. Hanks crazy sister and her husband, the Furry, Yoda, were visiting Hank for three days. (see "Nine Lives') Gloomer invited them over for a meal… she had never met a Furry…. or a Canadian.

I slept for four hours, then had the overwhelming urge to head outside. I missed the forest and the open fields, the pursuit of small furry rodents and the horny trailer park Queens. I got to the big maple tree in the meadow and looked up… there was old Slick, his butt plantified in the crotch of the tree- our Happy Place.

We had a great few hours… mousing, ratting, chasing rabbits terrorizing voles (bad dining alert!), chasing barn swallows (tasty) and, of course, catching up on our Christmas backlog of Horny Queens.

We were dynamite in the consexual coitus department… we both got 10 stars out of 5 on our Yelp review. As we lay on the skanky carpet in front of Hank's little wood stove, exhausted from our hunting and procreation, I remarked to Slick, "Pope Benny would be proudified."

I headed back to the manshun for some rest. Rosa had left me out egg-nog with some rum… I had a helluva sleep. At lunch time, Afrodite, looking like she was right outa Vague magazine rounded up Goldenboy, me and Gloomer to go down to the Christmas brunch at Sven's Yogi and Spa. The Pope posters had arrived from Amazon (what could they not do?) The goddess took a few posters to hang at Sven's Spa… Sven looked amazing… in a bright red stretchy body suit with flashing lights around his neck and Reindeer antlers. His carrot and gonads were looking fabulous with the correct N-S-E-West geographic orientations.

All of the Sven Sexy Seven showed up to the brunch… with some unruly teenagers (from 1st husbands) and infants (from 2nd husbands). Of course, they were all looking amazing as they snacked on little bits of turkey and healthy salads. The regular suburpinite yogi women were chowing down mashed potatoes, turkey dressing and gravy followed special Scandalavian Christmas cookies and chocolate Turtles.

Sven gave a nice little speech, "Vell, ladies, ze last few veeks haf been some of zee tuffist in my life… But

I have ze brand new , jumbo artificial left testacle… and I am ready for ze bugie again. So, ladies, ve are back in ze business!"

Everyone cheered as Sven did thirty-five jumping jacks in the middle of the mat. We hung our poster up on the wall and everyone admired our picture with Pope Benny. The Sven Sevan had a great re-union… all wearing their new designer sweat suits and head-bands…they had a good chuckle remembering Sven's un-doing by being kicked in the go-nads by Tootsie Trammel's size 10 Jimmy Choo shoe. ('Nine Lives.')

The Sven Seven actually awarded Tootsie a golden Karate Kick trophy for that move…Tootsie had tears in her eyes. Sven was hiding in the office… talking to his PTSFD therapist for support.

When we got back to the manshun at about four o'clock. Freeda, Hank, and Yoda were coming over for supper.

Rosa announced, "A la mierda. Estoy pidiendo pizza para la cena. Maldito Canadiense que piensa que es un maldito beagle." ("Fuck it. I am orderering pizza for supper. Goddam Canadian who thinks he is a Beagle!" Rosetta's Stones.)

V-Dome did not show up for supper. Michaela, his store #57 manager, phoned to say that Big Little Vinnie, the boss, had come up from New Jersey for a business meeting. At the moment, V-Dome was "tied up!". She was hoping to negotiate his release… Big Little Vinny had made V-Dome "an offer that he couldn't refuse" for his chain of 57 Starstuds and More coffee shops.

At that moment our company arrived at the vaulted front entry of the manshun. Everyone shook hands and exchanged greetings,

"Hey, I'm Freeda from Niagara Falls, Aye."

"This, here, is my useless husband, Mike, who thinks he is a friggin beagle called Yoda, Aye."

Yoda, who was six feet tall on his hind legs, was wearing quite a striking brown, black and white velour beagle suit with brown floppy ears, a long wet, pink tongue, and a tail that pointed up. He had a dirty, spitty, tennis ball in his mouth. Yoda mumbled, "Woof, woof! Aye!" around the tennis ball.

A Furry was an otherwise normal human bean who adopted an animal 'Fursona' and enjoyed dressing and acting like that animal to the point of, at times, believing that he or she was, in fact, a member of that genus. (cat, dog, beaver, armadillo, skunk etc.)

Hank walked in, wearing a new Christmas sweater with Santa on it and said, "Howdy."

Me and Slick, Goldenboy and Gloomer took Yoda outside to throw the tennis ball for a while. Hank and Freeda went into the kitchen to have a few Buds with

Rosa to wait for the Pizza. Afrodite worked out on the nearby exercise bike, sipping a Diet Coke.

Yoda was the clumsiest damn Beagle in the universe. He could not see properly through his eye holes… so he kept running into the black metal fences and gates… ouch. Also, he kept tripping over either his tail or the tennis ball. It was embarrassing. So Slick and me chasified a few rabbits over to him and he growled, pretending to catch them in his jaws and shake them. In fact, those rabbits have never been safer in their lives. We let the bunnies escape to thank them for playing along with the gag.

The Pizza arrived from Amazon (what can't they do) and me and Slick and Yoda had pepperoni, ham and shared a Bud in a bowl on the floor. Yoda gobbled up his food in 3.5 seconds and slurped down two beers and then greedily eyed our meals. Slick had to bite him in the ass twice. At one point Yoda tried doing 'tricks' to earn more supper. The six foot beagle looked ridiculous begging and rolling over for more peperoni. Finally he started yodelling "Eidelviess" for attention… which was not too bad. Afrodite took a big handful of peperoni and tossed it outside and scolded Yoda, "Look, asshole, you are not a fucking Beagle. Grow up!"

He was whining outside on the front porch for most of the rest of the visit.

When Freeda and Hank left at about 7:30 PM, Yoda was gone. Slick figured he had decided to walk back home to Sleep Safe Trailer Park. Freeda and Hank graciously thanked Afrodite and Gloomer and Goldenboy and Rosa for the hospitality. Gloomer gave them a coupla posters of the crew with Pope Benny. Freeda, being a JWyah, probably burned her poster.

Slick and me had a few glorious hours on the lam after dark… but we were still jet-lagged. We took several more serious steps to remedify the oversurply of horny Queens. We never did see Yoda.

According to Slick, the dog catcher for Fox Chapel Hill Gated Community picked up Yoda and put him in the dog pound for 'no dog collar and public urination'. Freeda decided to leave him in the slammer for a few days before paying the fine.

The following morning, V-Dome had not returned. Afrodite rounded up me and the two teenagers and we headed for Store #57… the scene of the crime. Afrodite lugged along a Pope poster as a justification for the trip. Sure enough, V-Dome's red Porch convertible was parked behind the store in 'the Boss Spot'. We went in the back door. Michaela was managing the store and pointed downstairs to the basement. We knocked and three hoarse voices yelled "The fuck ya want?"

As we descended the stairs we could see V-Dome under a bright light being lashed by one of the Tonys (Big Tall Tony, I think) with long strands of soggy spaghetti. Their boss, Little big Vinnie, a swarthy man with a crroked hook of a nose and psoriasis on his face, said, in a nasal gangsta voice, "We are the Pasta gang and we are making your husband an offer he can't refuse. If the spaghetti doesn't break him, we will work up through fettucine, penne, rigatoni all the way to the frozen lasagna."

Big Tall Tony whipped V-Domes bald head with spaghetti with a bit more gusto. V-Dome struggled bravely against his restraints. Afrodite asked Big Little Vinni,

> "Are you part of the Mafia … muscling your way in on the Starstuds chain?"
>
> Little big Vinnie laughed, "No, sister, we are the Mafia Lite… we want is to run all the 'More' rooms. Cash business. The Mafia Lite launders mob money… we are bankers… not thugs."

V-Dome's 'More Rooms' allowed two patrons privacy in a small room with a clean bed for $20 for ten minutes. It was his greatest business idea… V-Dome had 120 More Rooms working in his chain. They were yielding close to $100,000 daily gross. The Mob planned to double the price.

Afrodite motioned Big Little Vinnie over to a small table and yelled at Goldenboy, "Hey kid, get us a round of expressos, will Ya?"

Goldenboy and Gloomer headed up to the coffee shop. Afrodite untied V-Dome and stuck his Nordic Blond wig back on the Velcro strip. Someone had ripped his new hoop earring out of his right earlobe. V-Dome cast foul looks to Big Little Vinnie, Big Tall Tony, Skinny Horny Tony and Hungry Fat Tony and said,

"You guys can't torture worth shit."

Vinni shrug, "Hey, we are bankers. Whadya expect, waterboarding?"

Afrodite appeared to be the only negotiator at the table with working brain cells. She quickly sketched up an agreement:

1. The 'More Rooms' would be run …for cash… by the Mafia Lite. The price would go up to $20 per person per 10 minutes of private 'Luv Time." In return, the Mafia Lite would pay V-Dome and Afrodite $100,000 USD cash per month for use of the More rooms and the opportunity to launder Mafia cash through the registers of the 57 chains stores. The Mafia Lite would install '6 for 5' token machines in every store. 'More' tokens would sell for cash only… costing a $20 bill for 1 token or a $100 bill for 6 tokens. The Mafia Lite wanted cash money… they would have it.

2. V-Dome would control and run the coffee shops as before and would retain ownership and control of employees. Mafia Lite thugs had to call V-Dome "Mr. Woodbridge" or "Boss"… not Rughead.

3. Skinny Horny Tony had to apologize to V-Dome for tearing out his hoop earring with spaghetti that was too al dente.

4. The Mafia Lite would keep undesirables… hookers, druggies, and other thugs away from all the stores. Mafia Lite members could drink free caffeinated beverages in any store, but had to pay for food. (V-Dome was hung up on all the free food that Hungry Fat Tony was eating.)

V-Dome stopped seeing himself as a victim and smiled and shook hands with Big Little Vinnie and the three Tonys.

Vinnie looked at Afrodite in awe, "Hey, sister, we need someone with a sharp mind to run a Republican political campaign in Pennsylvania for us in the 2024 Presidential Race. Interested?"

Afrodite thought, "Who is the candidate? Not that asshole, Rump, I hope."

Vinnie said, "No. It's Ronnie DeSanta From Florida! God chose him!"

Afrodite asked, "Really? That tool. What does it pay?"

Vinnie said, "Political money is soft and gooey. How about a million for two years and a half years?"

Afrodite giggled and nodded, and muttered quietly, "Assholes! There is one more born every minute. I will get back to you on that offer."

V-Dome looked like he swallowed a canary. His whip marks would take minutes to fade. He had driven a hard bargain.

Chapter 13

Opa Visits Fox Chapel Hill

"When you are born you get a ticket to the freak show. If you are born in America, you get a front row seat."
—George Carlin

Opa Windfree had been hounding our agent for an interview ever since I got knighted in the Papal Order of the Golden Sperm. An exclusive interview with Me, Goldenboy, Gloomer, Hank and Slick was planned at the manshun in Fox Chapel for the upcoming Saturday. Pope Benny LXXXIV, who had got unbelievable PR outa the whole 'Golden Sperm' knighthood deal planned a "surprise visit" during the interview. Opa, who had visions of soaring ratings, approved the Pope's visit. Pictures of my junk being knighted had gone viral around the world again.

Donald Rump had declared himself as "Pro-Sperm and Pro-Cat." Ron DeSanta was quoted, saying, "I am on the fence when it comes to tomcats."

About two hundred TV folks showed up at the manshun early Saturday morning. Almost all of them had "Gripper" on their name tags. Golden boy set up Speechify for me on a low table in the sunroom where the light was good, so that I could converse with Opa. Goldenboy proudly displayed the huge Golden and Silver jock strap cup trophies from Shaq and LeBron ('Nine Lives') in the sunroom. (Our booty from the East Coast Sinus Fair at Harvard.)

Opa had asked me for one really good joke … then a discussion on cat humor, cat intelligence, religion and, of course, sperm. Goldenboy and Hank hoped to sing 'On the Road again' with Gloomer on Banjo. Slick and me had rehearsified 'Crying', by Roy Orbison… but we were flexible. Hank got $500 bonus from his boss for wearing his mid-blue Amazon ball cap and sweatshirt with swooshes on them. Slick refused to be cheapened by commercialism. He wore his red Cardinal's hat. (galero.)

Opa arrived by helicopter in the snow at noon. We had some expresso and got settled in the sun-room. No wonder Opa was America's sweetheart… she was gracious and friendly and super smart. Starting the interview, Opa said, "Hey, Sir Felix… start us out with a yuk-yuk!"

Ever the showman, I put on my silver cape and red cardinal cowboy hat (galero). My fingers flew over the keyboard and Morgan Freedom boomed out of the sound system:

"Hello, this is God… telling a joke:" Everyone laughed.

"A priest, a rabbi and a lawyer were playing golf. There were dark storm clouds boiling above them in the sky. All three golfers had a tricky shot over a pond onto a raised green. The priest swung and splashed his ball into the water and said "Shit, I missed!"

The rabbi swung twice and splashed two balls in the water and said, "Shit, I missed twice."

The lawyer picked up his ball and threw it over the water onto the green. It rolled up to within one foot of the pin. The lawyer said, "That's a gimme."

Suddenly, black clouds rolled in and crashing thunder rumbled. A huge fork of lightening split the air and fried the priest and the rabbi. There were just two pair of golf shoes left with wisps of smoke where the priest and rabbi had stood. The lawyer looked stunned.

"A deafening deep, booming voice echoed over the golf course, "Shit, I missed, twice!"

The whole gang had a good belly laugh including Rosa, who was sitting next to Opa. Opa spoke pretty good Spanish.

Opa put on her most intelligent voice and looked at me, "Sir Felix, First Knight of the Papal Order of Golden Sperm, is the crown a heavy one to wear?"

I answered in Morgan Freedoms voice, "Sorry, Opa, no crown, no sword, no shield , no horse... nothin!...Just a few taps on the gonads with a butterknife, a trip around Italy... which was great, and 5 crappy Papal T-shirts. And pictures of my junk plastered across every website in the galaxy."

Opa blushed, "Are you not happy being a knight?, Sir Felix?"

I answered, "Yes, Opa, it has been a thrilling experience. I love the Pope, who is a cat-lover, However, I am being paparazified to death every time I go outside to pee. And now, everyone wants my Golden Go-nads as Catholick relics when I die. Each of my go-nads has a hundred thousand Euro bounty on it!"

Opa sighed, "Tell me about it. Some days I just want to go out to my garden and pull weeds. The press are too much, too much by far."

She gave the nearest camera a big smile and wink. Just then, there was a tap at the sliding patio door leading to the snowy back yard.

There stood Afrodite, looking georgeous in a soft purple "Ron DeSanta for President" sweatshirt. Next to her was V- Dome, his Nordic Blond wig freshly combed wearing a 'Starstuds and More' Sweatshirt. Gloomer let them enter, on camera. As if they had just discovered they were parents, the dramatic couple rushed into the room to hug and kiss their children and Rosa and me, on camera. They both hugged Opa and shared (on camera) that she was their favorite celebrity on earth. They were honored, no… blessed, to have her visit. With more hugs and kisses, they departed back outside.

Before Opa could ask another question, Pope Benny arrived at the front door, entering with his entourage to press the flesh with Opa and crew. Benny was looking very dapper, all dressed in red with a galero to match me and Slick. On camera, he thanked me, Sir Felix of the Golden Go-nads for being a pillar of rectitude for catholicks and cats around the world. He explained that being 'Pro Sperm" was becoming the new 'woke status' in Europe.

Opa begged Hank and Goldenboy and Gloomer to sing "On the Road Again"… to shut the Pope up. They did a fine job. Gloomer was excellent on the banjo.

The Pope finally excused Himself, "I got to go to Philli. Dos preests, have been slippink der hands in ze cookie-jar again. Dos Rascals. Vaat a job, like baby-sinking."

Opa launched another question, this time at Goldenboy, "Goldenboy, how have you coped with the fame and notoriety of teaming up with such a famous

Tomcat. First the ground-breaking science at Harvard... then the Papal knighthood?"

Goldenboy stretched, "Well, Opa, it has been a blast. We have had so much fun. In Venice, we experienced a speedboat race in a movie with Tom Cruiser and The Rock. I loved it! And later, we got to shoot real AK-47s at real Somali Pirates. In Europe, at twelve, I can drink wine and beer."

Opa winced.

At that very moment three little darling, toe-headed kids, who were standing in the snow outside, started pounding on the sliding door. Gloomer let them in... "Who the hell are you?"

They sprouted huge smiles, did a little dance, and announced theatrically, to the cameras, "We are Minnie, Mickey and Mimi DeSanta... our daddy is running for President and our mommy, Tracy, is Cuuuu...ute!"

Sure enough, Ronny and Tracy DeSanta, in the flesh, leaped through the open slider door into the sunroom, in front of the cameras, paragons of wholesome American pulchritude (beauty).

"Hi folks, we were in the neighborhood to see our Pennsylvania campaign manager." At this point Afrodite also jumped through the door again from outside in the snow. After more extensive hugs, kisses and sincere handshakes... the children and their parents cleared out. The kids really were cute (poor little bastards.) Pictures of

Opa and the Desanta kids spread virally around the galaxy within seconds.

By this time Opa had totally lost the plot and said, "Hmmm. I think we got enough. Felix, did you say you and Slick can do, 'Crying'?"

I love Roy Orbison. So we sang 'Crying" with as much emotion as a Tomcat can muster on short notice. Opa sprouted some genuine tears while we sang. We bid fond farewells to Opa and crew.

When we stepped outside the Sven Sexy Seven, the entire chapter of Pittsburg Hell's Angels, plus the Richview High School Marching band were performing "West Side Story" in our driveway in 10 inches of snow.

Tootsie Trammel had intimidated her way into the role of "Maria". Sven was playing the demanding role of 'Tough Guy with Slicked-Back Hair #12'. Sven played his role with gravitas, although he kept slipping and falling down on the icy driveway.

Opa's helicopter left in a huge cloud of snow. We put on warm coats and stood outside to watch the grand finale of the musical where the Jets and the Snarks became good pals and opened a community skateboard park and pub.

The Satan's Choice guys were a bit heavy (overdramatic), but excellent at stomping. Tootsie Trammel, as Maria, was "Exhilarating in the lead female role."

Chapter 14

Las Vegas or Bust... or Both

"If you hope to leave Las Vegas with a small fortune, go there with a large one."—Anon

On Monday, after school, Goldenboy presented me and Gloomer with another exciting opportunity. "So, guys, we have the chance to go to Vegas for a month and live with Tenn Garrett… the famous tall guy in Tenn and Peller, the magicians who have headlined in Vegas for at least 30 years. We would stay with his family at their ranch on the edge of Vegas. He has a 12 year old son and a 16 year old daughter."

He continued, "During the day, I would work at UNLV (University of Nevada Las Vegas) with a brilliant Newtonian Physicist called Hermann Huptsnaud… a distant cousin of Tenn Garrett. He specializes in flight analysis and creates stunts for Hollywood movies and acrobatic work for Cirque Du Soleil. He also designs car and motorcycle stunts for Robbie Knievel Jr., Evel Kievel's talented grandson. I can get 3 Advanced Placement Science Credits and write up my scientific paper from our Harvard studies with Dr. Huptsnaud. We would stay in Vegas for one month. If we love it, we can go back for the summer."

Goldenboy looked at me, and continued, "Tenn and Peller need you for a 15 minute stand-up spot to warm up their audience for the 9 PM show. They also want to use you to appear in a 'disappearing illusion' early in the show each night." One show at 9 PM Wednesday through Saturday only. $2500 a show plus free room and board and travel. I get $800 a show for managing the act."

Goldenboy looked at Gloomer, "Hope, you could attend high school in Vegas and get paid as an assistant to Felix in the comedy/magic performance. $400 a show."

Gloomer smiled and nodded, saying, "What a sweet gig."

I said via John Wayne, Speechify, "Two conditions, pardner. Slick and Hank are gonna wanna come along… And, we keep a suite at the Rio Hotel and Casino where the show is hosted, in case we get kinda tard of the Garrett family."

Me and Goldenboy high-fived. What could possibly go wrong?

I met Slick after dark at our Happy Place. There was quite a bit of snow, so we chased a few rabbits by tracking them. The mice and rats mostly retreated to the barn for the winter. It was great to be back on the hunt. It was easier to spot owls and hawks in the winter without leaf cover. Me and Slick were keeping a close eye on our life totals (5 ½ years) and our go-nads… not wanting to get converted into a religious relic. (Slick had little risk of being relicified, but believed himself to be somewhat vulnerified by association with moi.)

We had a chat in Catonese about Vegas… Slick said, "Hell yeah, Vegas baby!"

Goldenboy was going to run it by Hank… good to have a token adult along.

The Queening had dropped off a bit… but, honestly, Me and Slick wore ourselves out on the Christmas backlog. Every few days Slick would say, "Kid, thank God I found you… I was headed for a young Hump Attack… no kidding!"

Hank told Goldenboy that he would love to go to Vegas with us… He arranged to drive for Amazon in Vegas for a month. Slick liked magic shows on TV and was looking forward to our gig. Magic without opposable thumbs is tough… especially card tricks. I worked hard on my list of good jokes and my Speechify skills. I could type

500 words a minute now on my iPad with added keyboard and electronic styluses velcoed to my front paws.

Trump and DeSanta had declared their runs for the 2024 Republican Leadership. After Afrodite got Ron DeSanta on Opa with his three oh- so-cute kids and his oh-so-cute wife, Tracy, Ronny was ready to make her his national campaign chairperson. Afrodite said she would do New York and Pennsylvania only… (for another million bucks over two and ½ years) because she wanted to stay close to her hairdresser, manicure specialist, yogi studio and her botox shooter. Ron empathized completely because he was also oh-so-cute.

Both V-Dome and Afrodite thought we should go to Vegas because it sounded like a 'sweet gig.' Rosa was happy to stay put and look after Goldenboy's menagerie.

We got an airport limousine to take us to Pittsburg Airport and caught a direct flight to Vegas. Tenn and Peller covered our flights and put us up in two connected swanky rooms at the Rio Suites Hotel and Casino (where the Tenn and Peller Theatre was located).

Goldenboy and Gloomer and me (and Hank and Slick… if they felt like it) could stay at the Garrett ranch (near UNLV) whenever we wanted. Hank was offered $300 per show to manage our A-V equipment (He had a stellar track record on button pushing!... 'Nine Lives.') The word was out in Vegas that I was opening for Tenn and Peller. Their tickets for the month sold out in one day (like Taylor Swifty). We flew on a Sunday to allow us a few days to get into the Vegas scene and get ready to perform. Tenn Garrett kindly welcomed us to his family ranch for supper.

The ranch sat on the edge of the desert on the way out to Red Rock Canyon. We immediately liked Tenn and his wife, Margie, a Vegas movie producer, and their kids ZaBuck (age 12) and Sadie (age 15). Goldenboy and Gloomer (Hope) warmed right up to them.

By the end of the visit we agreed that we would stay with them and use the hotel rooms, if needed, after shows. They had tons of room at the ranch. Me and Slick quickly scoped out the nearby desert. There were tons of desert rodents including some nasty rats. We were delighted to spot a nearby trailer park. We went to the hotel to sleep. In the morning we all went separate ways: Hank to Amazon to get an electric van, Gloomer to the high school near Sadie's house, and Goldenboy to UNLV to meet Dr. Hauptsnaud. Slick was having a day of leisure and I was working on my Stand-up routine. This was the major leagues. By the end of the day I mastered a solid 15 minutes of great quality humor. Slick giggled like crazy. Gloomer agreed to do my intro.

The Rio had engineered a cat-flap in our doorway… so me and Slick could move about freely. The staff in the buffet restaurant were happy to give us cream and bacon and tuna whenever we came around mewing. I was Sir GiGi and Slick was Slick. We enjoyed watching the look of surprise on the faces of moronic gamblers as the banks of one-arm bandits robbed them of their quarters. Once in a long while there would be a big hoopla when someone hit a 'Jackpot.' After that, every aunt from Topeka, Kansas would spend the next twenty minutes trying to muscle her way in to play the 'Lucky Machine.' Same old shit!

At about 5 PM Hank swung by and picked us up in a new Blue Amazon electric van with a big swoosh on the side. We zipped out to UNLV to pick up Goldenboy and meet Dr. Hauptsnaud from Heidelberg, Germany. He had a PhD in Rocket Science, but had been drawn to the glitz and glamour of Vegas. He was banned from all the casinos in Vegas as an unscrupulous Blackjack card counter. He was brilliant and had worked at NASA before being fired for betting against the Appolo Mission that crashed (told ya!).

Goldenboy introduced us to the frizzly-haired gentleman (like the old guy in 'Back to the Future.'... not Michael Fox) in a white lab coat with baggy jeans and sneakers. Dr. Hauptsnaud, stuck out his elbow for a bump and chuckled, "Yah! Pleased to meet yah!"

"This brilliant boy, Goldie, and I are going to do some vonderful science togezer. Ve are going to fly Robbie Knievel Jr. over ze Grand Canyon...on ze Indian Reservation... on a rocket/motorcycle in three veeks. Ve haf verk to do! Goldie you can bring ze cat in tomorrow wit you... I hear he is plenty schmart." Sounded interesting.

Goldenboy gave us a brief tour of Dr Hauptsnaud's rocket/motorcycle lab. A technician, Jerry, was tinkering with what looked like a mini plane with stubby wings and a short tail built on top of a Harley- Davidson motorcycle engine and chasis. The plane was about 10 feet long a 12 foot wingspan... painted a fluorescent baby blue, yellow and black.

Goldenboy was pumped about the canyon flight project... he and Dr. Hauptsnaud had filled a whole blackboard with numbers and equations to predict trajectories.

We had supper with the Garrett family. Margie, who was warm and welcoming, and a great cook, showed us the pool house in the huge back yard, which had three small sleeping area and a sitting area. It also had a cat flap...and access out through the fence to acres of open desert on the edge of the city.

Margie said, "It ain't fancy... but it is yours to use."

Sadie and Hope were hitting it off like besties already. Goldenboy and ZaBuck, who was also a science nerd, went to work in the garage where ZaBuck was building a robot that would cut grass. ZaBuck and Goldenboy were talking RAMs and Giga-bites and CPU's in a foreign language.

After supper, Goldenboy set me up with Speechify and Tenn and me and Goldenboy had a chat. Tenn and ZaBuck were fascinated by Speechify. They loved all the accents and voices and that I could type in speech at over 300 words per minute or just feed it printed text to read. I did God, Arnold , Darth Vader and John Wayne for them… they were wild about the possibilities. Goldenboy was a whiz with Speechify. I was working on pre-typing jokes into the Speechify program… and then lip-synching jokes at a mike like a real standup. (The mike had a start-stop button.)

Tenn said, "OK Felix… 10-15 minutes of good clean stand-up. It's a family show. Hope or Goldenboy can intro you. Hope could do a banjo tune…. maybe play 'Dueling Banjos' against herself while Goldenboy plays the spoons. Then me and Peller will disappear Felix a few times… it's funnier if it's a surprise."

Tenn could see he was dealing with pros. We had a few family games with the Garrett family, had a bedtime snack, and retired to the poolhouse. Me and Slick hit the desert for a couple hours of ratting and mousing… the Western rodent were fit and lean… but tasty. We heard a few rattlesnakes nearby.

In the morning, I went into UNLV with Goldenboy… he rode an electric bike (one of ZaBuck's) with me in a basket on the handlebars. Loved it!

Dr. Hauptsnaud and Jerry, the motorcycle/rocket technician were sculpting any excess fibre glass off the aerodynamic shape of the rocket/cycle. It was smooth as glass. They were perfectionists.

"Yah, make zat smoozer, Jerry. Und anozer layer of ze weneer glaze. It must be smooze. Ve need to fill zis little crevasse, yah."

"Ve project zat ze maximum shpeed is 275 miles per hour on ze take- off from ze 80 foot ramp. Zen, 425 feet over ze canyon and ze landing in ze sawdust bed on ze south canyon rim. Vat could go wrong? Ze math and ze physics are vonderful. Zis vill be ze longest motor-cycle jump in ze History."

At that moment, the pilot of the flying machine entered. He was about 25 years old, his thick hair in a bright red mohawk, with a bright red goatee. He had sparkling blue eyes and was wearing a red leather jacket and leather pants covered with blue stars. He carried a matching crash helmet under his arm. He had a thick cast on his left arm. In a husky voice, he said, "You can call me Evel Knievel the Third," and stuck out a fist to bump fists all around.

He grinned a blinding white smile. Evel Knievel III was the genuine grandson of Evel Knievel Sr., who won fame for amazing motorcycle stunts including jumping over the Fountains at Caesar's Palace in Vegas (141 feet), during which he crashed, fracturing his pelvis and femur (thigh), hip, wrist and both ankles… plus a concussion. He jumped the Snake River Canyon in a 'Skycycle-2" but the chute deployed prematurely and he fell short of the distant rim of the canyon. Multiple fractures. Over his dare-devil career, Evel broke as many as 443 bones (fun fact…the human body has 210 bones!)

Evel III had the same fearless attitude as his grandfather, "I said I was going to jump the Canyon, and I am going to jump the Canyon."

The National Parks service would not touch the jump… but Dr. Hauptsnaud was tight with the Havasupi tribal medicine man. The native tribe, an autonomous nation, who owed the land on a southern narrow branch of the Colorado River were keen for the income and promotion of their beautiful desert landscape. There were no paved roads in to the river canyon… but all of the major networks were interested and helicopters could fly hundreds or even thousands into the remote area to camp overnight.

Evel III was convinced he could make the jump with the lift from the wings and tail. Unfortunately, the flight pattern would have to remain theoretical until the day of the spectacular test of Evel III's courage and determination.

Dr. Hauptsnaud, with Goldenboy's help, crunched the data one more time with the pilot present. Dr. Hauptsnaud said, "Ze math is perfect. You vil fly over zat canyon. Do not gain any weight!" Goldenboy nodded.

Late in the afternoon, Me and Goldenboy and Slick went down to the Rio to set up for our first show with Tenn and Peller. We took the e-bike, a great way to travel around Vegas.

Golden boy set up the Speechify so that I could pre-enter my jokes and then do a true stand-up… lip-sinking the jokes in Morgan Freedoms voice by hitting a start-stop button on the microphone. We recorded and practiced 3 jokes… I was spectacular. Me and Slick also also practiced lip-sinked "Who Let the Dog's Out?"

We knew there was a Furry Dog convention in Vegas… there were literally thousands of 6 foot canines on the Strip as we drove through town. Apparently, the hospital ER's kept sending Furries (the 6 foot Beagles and Labradors… who were being hit by cars at an alarming rate) to the Veterinary Hospital… and the Veterinary Hospital kept sending them back to the human hospitals.

We e-biked back to Tenn Garrette's place and had a great supper and evening with his family. Gloomer was wild about Sadie… they were like sisters. Goldenboy and Zabuck chatted excitedly about the canyon flight and shared the math and physics calculations.

On Wednesday, I perfected my standup with the microphone. I had chosen to wear my silver cape and my red boots and my red Cardinal's hat.

When we arrived at the Rio Theatre, the placed was packed. At least two-thirds of the seats were full of Furries… Beagles, Rottweilers, Poodles, Dashunds,

Labradors, Collies, … even a few dwarves dressed as Corgis.

Gloomer opened with a stirring rendition of 'Dueling Banjoes" (playing both parts… she was officially a banjo prodgidy.) Goldenboy played the spoons along with her. The crowd loved them, woofing enthusiastically.

Goldenboy introduced me, "Tonight Tenn and Peller are delighted to introduce the first and only Stand-up Tomcat… famous on social media. Here he is folks, The first Papal Knight of the Golden Sperm, Sir Gigi… Felix the Tomcat." Thunderous applause.

I stood on my hind legs in my red boots, silver cape and red Cardinal's Galero (mini cowboy hat) with the microphone in both paws… so I could easily work the start-stop button for Speechify.

I lip-synched along with Morgan Freedom's booming voice, "Hi there, This is God talking." Everyone howled with laughter.

"A teenage girl brings her boyfriend home to meet her parents. He is wearing a leather motorcycle gang cut, and has tattooes on his face and neck and a gold chain from his nose to his right ear. He speaks in grunts. After he leaves, the mom says,

"I'm not sure that he is a very nice person, dear."

The daughter looks defiantly at her mom, "Then why is he doing 500 hours of Community Service?"

The crowd loved it. Slick joined me and we lip-synced "Who let the Dogs Out?" with Gloomer on the banjo and Goldenboy on the spoons. The crowd went bananas on the chorus, "Woof, woof-woof!"

"A rabbi, a priest and a Baptist preacher were at a rural hotel eating supper together. They got into a heated discussion on who was better at making converts to their faith. They decided on a challenge… Each of them would go into the surrounding woodland and find and convert a wild bear to their religion. They all set out at dawn the next day.

They met again for supper the next day… The Baptist Minister, who had both arms in casts, reported, "I found my bear fishing for Salmon in the river… He knocked me down and broke my arms… but I managed to baptize him."

The Catholic Priest, who had crutches and casts on both legs, said, "Well I chased my bear up a tree and got a rosary over his head and said three 'Hail Marys' before he pushed me out of the tree, 20 feet off the ground. Broke both my legs in seven places."

The Rabbi got wheeled in for supper in a hospital bed… all four limbs in traction, in a complete body cast. He mumbled "Maybe I shouldn't have started with the circumcision.""

The Furries and regular folks were loving it! Everyone was cheering and barking.

"Did you hear that Tenn Garnett got a new Corvette convertible and asked a priest, a Baptist Preacher and a

rabbi to come out to his ranch to bless his new car. The Priest hung a rosary from the rear-view mirror and said 6 'Hail Mary's' to bless the car. The Baptist preacher washed and waxed the car. The rabbi took a hacksaw and cut two inches off the tail-pipe."

The audience howled. Dramatic intro music filled the auditorium and a booming Morgan Freedom voice said,

"This is God again…introducing your favorite Las Vegas Magicians, "Tenn and Peller!"

The stars of the show arrived, asking me to stay on stage. The had me sit in a little throne in the middle of a wide table they used for card tricks. Tenn was wearing a top hat which made him 7 feet 7" tall. (He was 6' 7".) After some slight of hand tricks with cards… Peller, who not speak during the act but had great body language humor, scratched his head and pointed at me. Tenn threw something in my direction that created smoke and fire… but I did not disappear. He did that three more times… but I just remained sitting in the chair. I pretended to check my watch and Peller pointed at Tenn and laughed.

Finally, Tenn put his top hat over me then picked it up and put it back on his head. As he covered me with the hat, a trap door in the table opened and me and the throne dropped through the table into a room below the stage. An assistant grabbed me and strapped a parachute to the top of the throne… and put a safety belt on me. Next thing I knew I was high above the stage on a platform holding the stage lights.

In spite of my vigorous objections I was hurled skyward and the parachute snapped open. I drifted down, landing back on the Magicians' table… with enthusiastic applause.

Our whole gang, Me, Slick, Goldenboy, Hank and Gloomer stayed to watch the 90-minute show which was clever, funny and very entertaining.

At the end, Tenn and Peller and the whole crew congratulated us… "That was really good stuff. Purrfect!"

I was born for Vegas.

Chapter 15

Rocketry 101

"I never think of the future. It comes soon enough."
—Albert Einstein

My stand-up work got smoother and funnier each night… for a cat with a hyperthymesified memory (I cannot forget anything!), 15-minutes of stand-up comedy was simple.

The on-off switch on the Speechify voice allowed me to speed up and slow down and pause for applause and laughter. The tickets for Tenn and Peller were the hottest tickets in Vegas… especially among Furries. On Thursday night we had a whole theatre full of Cat Furries… there were two patrons who, believing that they were lions, tried to eat the chef carving the beef at the buffet restaurant. The terrified chef tossed them the whole roast beef and escaped.

Me and Slick did Roy Orbisons' 'Crying' … we had 150 'Furry cats' crying and howling in unison… the Vegas Swat team paid us a visit. It was insane.

The day of the rocket/ plane/cycle flight approached rapidly. Me, Slick, Goldenboy, Evel III and Dr. Hauptsnaud rented a helicopter to fly out to the Canyon site on the Little Colorado River near Cameron, Arizona. The helicopter was fantastic and we flew over the Grand Canyon first. With rock walls, the Canyon was up to 6000 feet deep, 270 miles long and up to 18 miles wide. The Grand Canyon was amazing with castle-like pillars and columns of red and grey and gold and rust-coloured rock stretching skyward from the banks of the rushing white-blue Colorado River.

Evel III had chosen a good spot on the Little Colorado Canyon which was less deep (3200 feet) and narrower. The takeoff would be across the fairly flat western rim of the canyon and the landing would be in a massive pile of sawdust /woodchips on the eastern side of the river. Front-end loaders were building the 800 yard road and 100 yard smooth take-off ramp (elevated at ten degrees) leading up to the western edge of the canyon. Sawdust had been arriving for a week via a rough road on the reserve and there was a massive pile heapified on the east side of the river. After a long flight (400 + foot) over the canyon, the plane/cycle/rocket would descend slowly with a parachute into the sawdust mountain. After the initial burst of engine power to become airborne… Evel would be gliding across the canyon. We got out and walked the site.

Evel felt that it was "A pieca cake." And so the next few weeks went... show business and rocket business. Me and Slick had some amazing nights on the prowl. We ran into that obnoxious coyote that ate us... Wilie, who chased a roadrunner by us going 120 miles an hour in the desert. He had a rocket pack strapped to his back... Wilie must have gotten his Amazon credit card back.

We stalked a few Arizona desert Pack Rats who are large, nasty rodents with long furry tails and a white belly. Bobcats and owls also dine on desert Pack rats... so we kept a careful lookout. Slick and me were guarding our lives and our go-nads. We also found the trailer park and some horny Queens. However, there were two Mobbed- up (made) Tomcats who worked as bouncers at the Wynn casino hanging around. So, we jumped in for a couple quickies and called it quits. Family life was rich... Goldenboy and Gloomer loved having 'parents' who actually spoke to them and listened to them. Me and Slick loved the desert... I got to be a swimmer in the pool.

The day of the rocket/cycle/plane flight arrived. We headed out early on Sunday morning, hours before the stunt at 2 PM. A huge crowd was visible from the helicopter when we landed. All the networks were there: CNN, ESPN, Fox, NBC, MSNBC, and of course TSN and ESPN.

Evel was already there, sitting in an air-conditioned tent wearing a baby-blue leather suit covered with at least 50 red luminescent stars… with a matching helmet with full face shield. His arm cast was gone and his face looked thinner… maybe he was sick… or, god help us, scared. He was quiet.

The plane/ rocket/ cycle looked perfect… gleaming powder blue and yellow and black in the shimmering desert sun. Dr. Hauptsnaud, Evel and Goldenboy were interviewed to the point of torture by 22 talking heads from all the networks plus 23 independent indie-movie makers who had an average age of 11 ½. In a nutshell, Evel III explained,

"Shit yeah, the sucker can fly off a ramp and crash into sawdust!"

As 2 PM approached, Dr. Hauptsnaud kept looking at Evel. Finally, he asked… "Evel the Turd, How much veit haff you lost?"

Evel III looked embarrassed and said, "Between the arm cast and anxiety and diarrhea… 24 pounds!"

Dr. Hauptsnaud took out his computer and did rapid calculations… "Zat vill not verk. Wizzout zat 24 pounds you vill climb and climb and go into ze low earth orbit. No, No No! Shit!"

Evel III echoed "Shit!"

Dr. Hauptsnaud said, "No! No more shit!"

Golden boy and Dr. Hauptsnaud ran around weighing stuff… including me and Slick.

"Ve need ballast for ze flight that can self-eject if necessary. A bag of ze dirt vill not do ze job."

And so, me and Slick became assistant pilots on the infamous Little Colorado Canyon stunt by Evel Knieval III. We had to sit on Evel's lap in the cockpit, wearing what Dr. Hauptsnaud said were 'mini-parachutes'.

A brass band from the Hopi reserve showed up and played "Amazing Grace" and "Abide With Me." I asked them for something more up-temp so they played "Memories" from 'Cats'.

The cycle/plane/rocket was elegant, with swept back wings and a working tail for steering up and down and side to side. The wings rested on lightweight struts with lightweight wheels to keep the plane upright on two Motorcycle wheels until we were airborn.

The plane/ cycle/ rocket was seriously loud as we sat at the end of the smooth dirt takeoff road leading up to the ramp. The huge Harley-Davidson 131 Crate Engine, expertly mounted on a titanium frame with big wheels and suspension, roared like a lion as Evel III gunned the engine. Dr. Hauptsnaud came up with final instructions,

"Ze cats will have to jump out if ze crash is happenink!"

Evel III said, "Whaaa..." and hit the throttle hard while popping the clutch.

The cycle/rocket tore dwn the road and then up the sloped ramp toward the cliff ahead. The speedometer said 250 miles per hour. The world sped by as I realized that I had no crash helmet.

The plane/cycle/rocket soared upward off the ramp and began to deaccelerate with air friction. Evel III was howling with delight... can you say, 'Adrenaline Junkie'. Slick had wet himself and was screaming in terror. I was busy weighing our options. We slid through the still air surrounded by clear blue desert sky. The Little Colorado River and canyon stretched below us. Evel III maintained our elevation and steered for the massive pile of sawdust against the eastern wall of the canyon. The engine died and we could hear the wind whipping by our ears in the open cockpit. Evel III was still howling in delight... he was a certified psycho. (on the Y chromosome, I think!)

Suddenly, as our speed dropped, the nose of the plane pointed downward, not upward. We were headed for the sawdust pile at 200 miles per hour. Evel III hit the parachute button and the brakes suddenly went on, violently swinging the nose of the plane skyward. The plane/cycle parachute snapped open above us.

Me and Slick got ejected from Evel III's lap and flew through the air. Our parachutes were duds. I knew from our Harvard experiences ('Nine Lives') that my maximum downward velocity would be 60 mph ... but I was concerned about our forward velocity of 200 mph... heading for a canyon wall.

Fortunately, in spread-eagle positions, both me and Slick slowed down quite quickly and hit the soft sawdust on our feet (as every good cat must) in two huge plumes of sawdust similar to Hiroshima and Nagasaki. The crowd of thousands went nuts. The plane/rocket/cycle followed us catapulting into the huge mountain of sawdust.

Evel III jumped out and stood on top of the plane/rocket/cycle waving his arms in victory. Me and Slick stood on top of the sawdust, alive but shaken, and shook our fists at Dr. Hauptsnaud. Me and Slick deducted half a life each... "Shit." (5 lives to go.)

Evel III, Me and Slick all entered the Guiness Book of records as the longest motorcycle jump in History by Cats in the Winged category. Me and Slick also entered as cats with the highest drop from a winged motorcycle in History while remaining alive. (207 feet)

Our last night at the magic show was pretty hairy. There were three conventions in town: Furries who thought they were horses, Personal Injury Lawyers and the American Association of Sologomists (people who marry themselves). The horses were extremely clumsy and bulky and kept knocking into people at the bar before the show. Once horse spilled his drink and 16 lawyers and 4 Sologamists all hit the deck. They had to call the Las Vegas Swat Team to settle the combatants. Three of the Sologamists sued themselves for mental cruelty. The price for a "Horses Ass"... the back guy in a horse costume climbed from $200 to $300 per day and 3 horses got sued for farting in their partners face. It was a relief to tell jokes.

"A 50 year old lawyer dies and goes to heaven. He meets St. Peter and asks, "Why am I dead? I am only 50 years old?" St. Peter scratched his head and looked at the Book of Life and answered, "According to your billed hours you should be 106."

The horses and Sologamists loved that one. "And now a joke for you horses."

"A young musician went to the thoroughbred races. He looked carefully at all the horses in the first Race ... they all looked good. He noticed a really old Irish Priest blessing one of the horses with 40 to 1 odds. "Bless you my son, may ye run fast and well."

The priests's horse won by three lengths with 30 to 1 odds. The next three races were the same... the priest's blessing brought victory to the chosen horse.

By the fourth race the young man was betting the priest's chosen horses to win... with long odds. He multiplied his $50 dollars to $25,000 by the end of the eighth race.

For the final race he watched the priest praying carefully over horse #13 who had 100 to 1 odds. The priest finished off by anointing the horses head with holy water. The *young man raced to the betting window and bet $25000 on horse #13 to win the race.*

The horse ran last the entire race and barely made it over the finish line, and proceeded to have a cardiac arrest. Two jockies gave it CPR.

The young man confronted the old Irish priest, "What happened? All the other horses you blessed won their races."

The priest shook his head, "Me son, me son, don't ye know the difference between a blessin and the 'Last Rites'?"

The horse furries loved that joke and a few of them got up and tried to gallop around the theatre… but were tripped by the personal injury lawyers. More law-suits broke out. Two sologamists filed divorce papers.

I survived another drop from the ceiling with a parachute. The show was a remarkable success. We bid fond farewells to the cast and crew at the Rio… it was a sweet gig. Tenn and Peller and their families had become our true friends. We were invited back for two months in the summer, if we were free. We flew back to Pittsburg the next day.

Chapter 16

Politics as Usual

"Nearly all people can stand adversity, but if you want to test a person's character, give him or her power." —Abraham Lincoln

We were very happy to be back at the manshun in Fox Chapel Hill. Rosa had cooked a feast of Guacamolan food to welcome us home. Hank and Slick stayed for supper.

Afrodite looked georgeous, as usual, in a lime green velour track suit. She announced, "Family… I have an exciting new political job. I am leading the election team for Ronny DeSanta. My boss, Ron DeSanta, is leading the Republican polls for president. His appearance on Opa with his oh-so-cute wife and family swung the entire right wing behind him. Rump is now treading water at 18% and DeSanta has 47% of Republicans."

She beamed a smile and continued, "In a brilliant political move, his oh-so-cute wife, Tracy, has declared as a Democratic presidential candidate. Running with her maiden name, Tracy Rodriguez (Cuban parents) Tracy is a beautiful, smart, well-educated, east-coaster, news-show host. Jennifer Lopez meets Rachel Maddow. Joe Bide-one got confused in Europe and is running for Lord Mayor of London, England. Hilary finally divorced Bill and married herself (Sologamy) and is on a one-year world cruise with Sarah Palindrome. (also a Sologamist.) Even Bernie swore off talking and has gone on a hunger strike for a better pension. There is a Tracy-shaped vacuum at the top of the Democratic party."

Afrodite, gaining momentum, continued her soliloguy. I had no idea she was interested in politics. "Ron and Tracy could wrap up both party presidential nominations... everyone loves one of them. The winner seizes the presidency and whoever loses will be Vice-President. They can rule America for up to 16 years! Together, they could move the country forward. No more "politics as usual". And their three little guys are perfect... Minnie, Mickey and Mimi. They will campaign, as a family, together. With a big team of experts, I will be their manager and strategist. Opa will return to our house to interview the DeSanta team again in a week."

The other big change at the manshun was in V-Dome, who looked like a pudgy mini-Elvis. He was wearing a powder blue Elvis cape and jump-suit with 4 inch heel-lift, snake-skin cowboy boots and a slick-backed, black Elvis wig. The blonde goatee was history. He kept saying, "Thankyaverymuch, thankyaverymuch!"

He cleared his squeeky tenor rumble of a voice and unleashed a bad, off-key version of "Love me Tender" with lots of knee wobble and hip gyrationing. Finally, Afrodite poked him in the gut and said, "Shutup, asshole!"

That concludified the concert. He was performing at his 57 coffee-shops in rotation. He still had "Starstuds and More" badges stuck all over his Elvis outfit. He showed us his new canary-yellow Porshe 911 convertible in the driveway.

Rosa was excited to see us and gave all of us hugs, "Gracias a diosestes de Vuelta. Quiero mater a ese jodito gloton, Elvis." ("Thank god you are back. I want to kill that fucking greaseball, Elvis." Rosetta's Stones.) Goldenboy and Gloomer and me laughed heartily.

Goldenboy and Gloomer filled Afrodite and V-Dome in on the motorcycle stunt, Dr, Hauptsnaud, Ten and Peller and the magic show. Gloomer showed off her banjo progidy skills playing, "Dueling Banjoes." Goldenboy joined her on the spoons and Rosa did a Guacamolan folk dance. V-Dome shook his booty and shimmied around on high heels. Afrodite smiled with pride at her offspring and boogied along. It felt like a family. "Let's put the fun back in dysfunctional." (Felix the Tomcat)

Slick and me agreed to meet up after dark at our happy place.

It was a chilly February night with about two feet of packed snow. My warm rosettified coat kept me snug. Slick waited in the crotch of the maple humming Sousa's "Colonel Bogie March."

"Hey, kid. How are they hanging."

I checked and responded, "Golden, mate. And yours?"

Slick said, " All rested up and ready for action."

We had a wonderful night… field mice x5, rattus rattus x6, barn swallows x4 and we terrorized a ground hog who wandered by during a hibernation break. We were sharp of reflex and our jaws easily snapped through the skulls of our prey. We were alive. When we reached the Sleep Safe Trailer Park we had to hustle to satisfy all the Horny Queens seeking our acquaintance. We literally had to give IOUs to the last 6 applicants… we were outa juice.

Hank had left us big bowls of cream and tuna and bacon for a snack, which we scarfified before settling into a welcome pre-dawn naperoonie. This was 'Livin the Dream", writ large. On the way home I ran into a nasty feral Boxer Dog who thought he was "Rocky." Like most dogs called "Rocky", he could not climb worth shit… so 'no problemo."

Chapter 17

Opa Visits the Family

"They say: if you want a friend in Washington, get a dog." —Barack Obama

I had never seen Afrodite with any sense of purpose apart from being beautiful. She set up an office in my sunroom, which I enjoyed. She was smart and funny and had good ideas. She had a megabudget. Political dollars wanted to buy influence… she was playing both sides. Rich donors could not stop themselves jumping on the 'Santa-Rod' juggernut. Afrodite had hired a 30-year-old oh-so- cute personal assistance, Scotty, with a blond man-bun and big muscles like Sven. Scotty was not just a hunk… he was whip-smart and was finishing a political studies program at University of Pittsburg.

Afrodite, showing remarkable intelligence, appointed me, Goldenboy, Gloomer, Hank and Slick to join Scottie as her "Brainified Trust" to organize a "Common Sense Platform" for the political jugglernut she had pioneerified. V-Dome missed the cut.

At the first meeting, in the sunroom, we had a brilliant discussion on the topic 'What America needs now': With Scottie's bright leadership we quickly created a platform that was sure to get support from the right, the left and the middle from all citizens who thought their leaders were hopelessly swampified.

Sven had been admitted back to hospital when his 'Amazon billiard ball' went rogue and rejected him. Scotty had all his original parts in fine condition. Sven was replaced by Scottie on Tuesdays and Thursdays… and Saturdays and Sundays.

The Opa interview was kept a well-guarded secret… no "West Side Story" or marching bands allowed. Opa and her crew arrived by helicopter at noon. The 'Santa-Rod' team, with an entourage, arrived by tour bus from Florida. Afrodite had set up rallies for both candidates together in Philly, Pittsburg, Washington, Raleigh and Atlanta over the next 10 days to reveal "the Common Sense for America Party," a new American political choice.

Opa was bubbly and full of enthusiasm. She gave warm greetings and hugs to the group: me, Goldenboy, Gloomer, Afrodite, Slick, Hank, Scottie and the oh-so-cute DeSanta-Rodriguez Family- Ron, Tracy Rodriguez, and, of course, the extra-oh-so-cute Mimi, Minnie and Mickie all wearing matching 'Santa-Rod' sweatshirts and ball-caps.

Opa giggled and hugged the children, to start the interview. Mickie said, "My Mom, or possibly, my dad will be president! I will be the First Boy!"

That kid had 'politician' written on his fore-head!

Opa looked at me and said, "How are they hanging, Felix? How about a joke?"

I was ready with my new stand-up Speechify lipsink micropone, with the start-stop technique, "Opa, my go-nads are golden. Thanks for asking," I confessed, "I trust yours are also well."

Opa chuckled and blushed.

I put on the Morgan Freedom voice,

"Three contractors are bidding to fix the White House fence… one from Minnesota, one from Tennessee and one from Chicago. The White House Chief-of-staff shows them the fence.

The Minnesota contractor takes out a tape measure and a calculator. After 10 minutes of careful thought, she says $900… material $400, labour $400 and profit $100.

The Tennessee contractor does the same and she says $800… material $350, labour $350 and profit $100.

The Chicago contractor eyeballs the fence and smiles. He whispers in the White House officials ear… $3500… $1000 for you and $2500 for me… and I will hire that woman from Tennessee to fix the Fence for $800."

Everyone had a hearty laugh. Opa said, "Ok, folks, that describes what Washington is doing for us now. I understand that the 'Santa-Rod' team is offering something new and refreshing. She looked at Tracy Rodriguez, who gave her a beaming, shining white smile… Tracy was a beautiful, charismatic creature.

Tracy said, "Ronny and I are starting a new By the People, For the People (BPFP) Political Party" today… on your show. We are ready to lead this country back to Common Sense.

Ronny nodded thoughtfully, handsomely, toward the camera, his eyes showing steely determination mixed with a healthy dose of warmth and humility. He purposefully kept his mouth shut.

Opa said, "What will the BPFP Party platform be?"

Tracy said, "Afrodite?"

Afrodite smiled warmly and said, "Let me introduce our brilliant Political consultant, the Almost-Doctor Scottie McFarlane, an idealistic young genius who has raised and educated himself in West Virginia. He worked his way through 11 years of college by cleaning houses and selling firewood. He knows hard-work and he knows your pain.

Scottie flashed a huge smile with a mouthful of exquisitely-capped teeth and started, “Thank you, Opa. It is a privilege to work with Y’all.

I thank my gifted ‘Braniac trust’ who slavified many nights to create this platform for the new, Common Sense, BPFP Party. Our platform is:

1. Free health care for all. Health Care is a right… not a privilege.

2. Free child care for all children. Free up women to reach their true potential.

3. Free four year college tuition to all eligible students. Quality education is a right.

4. Ban all assault weapons… no one needs an AK-47 machine gun to hunt for rabbits or deer. Also ban open-carry and enforce background checks. We must stop the killing.

5. Introduce 8 year term limits on Senators and congress members. We must drain the swamp.

6. Impose a 10 year term limit on the Supreme Court. That swamp also needs drainage.

7. The top One percent of the world’s population owns almost 50 percent of the world’s wealth. The bottom 45% of the world’s population own 1% of its

wealth. We will apply a yearly 5% tax on the top one per cent of Americans yearly. This will raise 5% of 26 trillion or 1.3 trillion per year to pay for health care, education and immigration reform.

8. On immigration. Families with over $500,000 in assets, with a clean criminal record, would be granted immigration to the USA from any country in the world. We need diversity and we need workers. We would establish a quota yearly for legal immigration which would match the 'needed workforce' number of the previous year. Illegal immigrants and asylum-seekers would be allowed to stay and work from work-camps in the USA. Work camps would provide shelter, food, education, language classes, and health care and jobs at $10 per hour. After 5 years immigrants in work-camps could apply for legal immigration… if they were free of any criminal activity. The best immigrants would stay to become Americans.

9. The By the People, For the People party will be a new party, independent of Democratic and Republican control. Sitting congress and senate members have already approached us to join our new party. Let us, together, drain the swamp."

Ronny DeSanta finally spoke… "Opa, we would love to make you the first Honorary Chairperson of the BPFP Party. Would you consider that?"

Opa blushed and smiled, "Wow! Yes, I would. I would be honoured to stand with 'Common Sense," on three conditions: One, you and Tracy must show the ability to compromise and work together to show 'Common Sense' leadership to America. Two, You must name your next oh-so-cute kid Mopa … after me. Three, Felix the Tomcat does ten minutes of stand-up for your rallies, whenever possible.

Gloomer and Goldenboy finished up the interview with a banjo-spoons rendition of "Dueling Banjoes" and me and Slick and Hank and Afrodite did a little line-dancing. Opa said, "Wow! Great show!"

Of course, the Opa Interview flew around the world. The headlines on websites and Newspapers around the world read,

"Opa endorses new Common Sense BPFP American Political Party." (New York Times).

"Tracy Rodriguez-Ron DeSanta Team (Rod-santa) Promises a Refreshing New American Political Reality." (Washington Post).

"Felix the Tomcat Will be next US President" (Pravda… fake news).

Among Poles, Opa was always way ahead of Polish Sausage and liverworst.

Interestingly, Rump scheduled a rally in Pittsburg the same evening as the BPFP Rally. He figured he would show who was 'the man'.

Afrodite had booked the PPG Paints Arena (capacity 19,000). Rump was left with the Peterson Events center at the University of Pittsburg (capacity 12,000).

Unfortunately for Rump, a "Ticking Bomb" was discovered at his venue a half hour before his event... causing a two-hour delay in starting the rally. The "Ticking Bomb"was a diagnosed as a a 20 lb bag of Costco Brand "Chicken and Rice Formula Cat Food with Hairball Control," plus a red, 'Mickey Mouse' vintage wind-up alarm clock with loud ticking.

The 'Pittsburg Bomb Squad' was slow to respond due to five other 'Bomb Threats' received in the city that evening. Two of calls were to marijuana dispensaries... which totally stupified the sniffer-dogs'. The turnout for Rump was less than 5000 disgruntled fans... who booed him and called him, 'Ivan', which really ticked him off. Ivanka stood him up and Melena went to New York to go shopping. On camera, Chris Christy said "Donald who?"

Our Rally was a ginormous success. The Paint arena was packed (19,000) with 5000 fans outside watching a jumbo screen. I gave them a few old chestnut jokes to warm them up for the Rod-Santa team (Tracy was polling 55 to 45 over Ronny).

"A woman goes to heaven and meets God. She notices a broken clock sitting on God's desk and says, "What is with the broken clock?"

God says, "It is Mother Teresa's clock. It never moves- reminding me that Mother T. never ever lied."

The woman notices another old clock on the wall that just moves once in a while.

"What about the clock on the wall?" asked the woman.

"Oh, that is Barack Obama's White House clock… he just lied Occasionally," said God.

The woman notices a nice breeze in the room and points upward to the source.

God says, "Oh, that is Donald Rump's clock. It makes a good ceiling fan."

The huge audience killed themselves laughing. I gave them another:

"Did you hear that Donald Rump has quit eating Big Macs to watch his weight. We felt sorry for him and sent him some of my favorite catfood weighted with an alarm clock."

They chuckled, but it went over many heads. They would figure that one out tomorrow. I gave them another joke.

"A large group of brilliant scientists and neurosurgeons are experimenting to see if politicians need brains. So,

they take out half of Joe Bide-one's brain and ask him to count to ten.

Joe says, "One-3-5-7-9-10."

The scientists said, "Hmmm. No change."

Then they try a Republican and remove his entire brain and ask him to count to ten.

The politician says, "I can count bigly to ten. I am one of the best counters in the universe. I use the best numbers. The fake news lies about my numbers. I can count better than the Chinese. Everyone loves my counting. I have been invited to the counting Olympics. Ah… 1-3-10… I'm done."

The scientists confered and announced…"No change there either."

Ronny spoke first to the crowd. He was perceived as a bit of a cold halbut… so he pushed the humane, caring side of his personality… with success. He supported the new platform with enthusiasm to the delight of the huge, vocal crowd who were chanting "Common Sense, Common Sense, Common Sense."

Opa appeared via Zoom on the Jumbo monitor and voiced support and enthusiasm, "We need to drain the swamp. Government by the People for the People! Yes!"

Tracy batted clean-up and hit a home-run. As she revealed their hopes and dreams for the future of America, photos of their brilliant children Mickie, Minnie and Mimi flashed on the jumbo screen to the "Ooohs and aaahs' from the crowd, many with tears in their eyes.

She reviewed their brilliant "Common Sense...Drain the Swamp Platform of Ideas." The crowd loved it''' a politician making Sense!

By the next morning 95 congressmen (and women) and 22 senators had jumped ship to the new BPFP party. The media went crazy for the new party-BYFY and the new Team ... Rod-Santa . The couple quickly adorned the covers of Newsweek, Time, People and USA Today.

Even the National Enquirer picked up on it, "Felix the Tomcat is an Alien Politician from the Planet Wortzz who will take over the Country."

Nice to have a picture of my attractive face and body in the news for a change.

Editor's Comment: Words cannot describe my Golden Go-nad fatigue.

Arthur's Note: I have put my go-nads on the line for this literary masterpiece. You have risked what...? Writers cramp? Paper cuts? The writer explained... "Asshole!"

Chapter 18

V-Dome Changes it Up/Afrodite Moves On

The moment that Scottie appeared on the scene, the V-Dome-Afrodite connection was doomed to failure. Work and the Elvis gigs drew V-Dome to his coffee shops like a magnet. He also had found a 'Horny Queen' in the lovely form of Michaela who had been promoted to Vice-President of Coffee Operations and had taken over the red Porshe 911. They shared at penthouse condo in Pittsburg. V-Dome was focifying his energy on his Elvis work, including voice lessons. He still sang like shit. Every week Michaela organized a lottery for the 57 shops. The losing 5 franchises got a free concert from V-Dome as Elvis.

However, the Starstuds changes made everyone happy because everyone loved Michaela's calm, fair, inclusified manner. No one missed V-Dome and they all enjoyed yelling insults at Elvis. Starbuds and More was thriving. The cash-only 'More Rooms, now $40 per ten minutes,were going gang-busters with Big Little Vinny and the three Tonys at the helm. There were plans in place to open 13 more coffee shops by summer.

Afrodite and Scottie were a happy couple. Scottie, for a 30-year- old was mature beyond his years. Gloomer and Goldenboy found him funny and smart and interesting. He spent many hours helping Goldenboy with his natural animal sanctuary (they got a second Boa to mate with Bo).

He played guitar along with Gloomer's banjo... all her girlfriends found Scottie adorable. Afrodite was 'in love' and started singing ballads around the house. She had great 'diva star power' in her voice. Scottie moved in and V-Dome moved out! The manshun was a happy place.

The 'Brainiac Trust' met weekly in the sunroom to develop fresh ideas for the campaign. Hank lobbied Jeff Beznos, his boss, and soon Rod-Santa images were on every Amazon van in the USA ... with the'Common Sense' motto beneath. I spoke to Pope Benny in Rome and traded him my 'right nut' (after my ultimate death) as a Catholic relic (if I was not re-resurectified) in return for his promise to injectifying the words 'Common sense' into each of his speeches and sermons for two years. You could say I had skin in the game. Afrodite had charmed ten billionaires (so far) into supporting the BPFP by making them 'party directors'... (the illusion of power was intoxicating). Monthly, the 'Party Directors" met in Miami for a party and looked and felt important. Scottie and the 'Brainiac Trust' were calling the shots.

Scottie had become an expert in answering really tough questions...

> Question: "Should women have free choice on abortion?"
>
> Scottie: "Let me see... a tough and very personal issue. What would 'Common Sense' say? Whose life and whose body are we talking about?"

Scottie taught that skill to Tracy, Ronny and Afrodite... they never found themselves chewing on shoe-leather.

V-Dome and Afrodite decided to split up amicably... together, they had plenty... so they split it down the middle. We got the manshun and the Mercedes... V-Dome kept the coffee shops and the Porches and pledged $30,000 cash per month for alimony. Afrodite was happy, chatty and friendly and, at times, missed a manicure. Gloomer and Goldenboy were thriving with one parent who cared.

Hollywood embraced the BPFP Party instantly and everyone... from Brad Pitter to Angelina, to the

Rock, to DeNiro, to James Cordoron, to Meryl Strep, to Cher, to Madona, to Pee-Wee Herman was 'whoopin' it up' for 'Common sense'. You would think that 'Common sense' was a novel idea in the US. The Governor of Texas admitted, "It ain't necessary to shoot no AK-47 if ya just wanta kill a rabbit."

"Common Sensified" became the new 'woke status' around the world. The BPFP Party encouraged online donations of less than $1000.

Billionaires were allowed to rent venues for Rallies and cover travel expenses only. The time had come to seriously drain the swamp.

Me and Slick continued with our nightly adventures in the forests and fields. We now spent many thoughtful hours in the crotch of the maple thinking (our Happy Place) and planning America's future.

We were both 'outside the box' cats… so we often provided the spark to keep Scottie pushing in new creative directions. Hank, as a truck-driver, connected the "braniac trust" to reality. Even Afrodite, whose dad worked at 'Rolling Rock' re-connected to her roots.

Me and Slick excelled at our usual hobbies: ratting, mousing, terrorizing small mammals, and squirifying horny Queens… it was a sweet life. We would lie by hank's fire in the early dawn and strategize in Catonese until we drifted off to sleep.

This was quality living!

Chapter 19

How do You Spell Assasinate?

Of course, there was a tremendous backlash to the new "Common Sense Party." Rump and the KKK and the Oathkeepers called us "Commies." The 'Back to Nature Lefty Party' types called us "Fasciists." But most people said, "It's about time those political ass-holes woke-up!"

Rump's popularity among Poles had dropped from 35% to 3.5 % ... he was behind Spam and just ahead of head cheese. He was desperate. He was losing hair and turning deep burnt orange. Jared had disowned him and Ivanka's kids were refusing to call him "Grampa Mr. President." (his chosen grandpa name).

Last night, while gallavantering, me and Slick noticed a shadow following us around as we executed rodents and screwified horny Queens. Slick said, "Kid, I think we got company."

But, no attack came. I thought I caught a whiff of rancid coyote in the breeze. We attended a rally in Washington the following evening, riding down on the Rod-Santa bus with the whole team. Gloomer and Scottie played folk songs and Ronny, Tracy and Afrodite sang Harmony. The oh-so-cute DeSanta kids sang "It's a small World" twenty-four times in a row until we stopped for a Dairy Queen.

As we walked from the tour bus to the entrance of the Capital One Arena (capacity 20,000) we were feeling rested and confident. Suddenly, there was a loud "WHOOSH," SWOOSH," … "CRASH" … KABOOM!...and what appeared to be a rocket ripped off the front of our bus and blew a large piece of concrete off the front of the building. A hundred yards down the road a skinny coyote dusted himself off, stamped his feet a few times and stalked off.

He could barely carry his FGM-148 Javelin Missile Launcher (Amazon $174,000). Whoever was funding that Coyote hit-man had mucho deep pockets. Ron DeSanta, being an ex-Navy Seal lawyer said,

"I am going to sue that fucking coyote."

Tracy said, "I am going to kill him," and they swept the three little oh- so-cute Mickey, Minnie and Mini off to safety.

Me and Slick tailed the coyote for a few blocks till he got in a black limousine and said, Rump Hotel." Wilie Coyote was also packing a Smith and Wesson 500 Magnum Snub Nose revolver (Amazon$1500) in a shoulder holster. Obviously, Wilie did not realize that Washington, D.C. prohibified open carry (unlike Nevada.)

Someone… someone who knew Wilie Coyote, with a lot of money, was out to kill or maim the Rod-Santa BPFP Team, including me).

The death threat increased the buzz about the BPFP Party and both Tracy and Ronny gave wonderful inspired speeches. Tracy asked,

"What does Common Sense say about a mangy coyote in the middle of Washington with a Rocket launcher and a 50 caliber pistol?"

The crowd of 25,000 screamed, "Ban assault weapons, Ban assault weapons!"

One geek was yelling, "Ban coyotes!"

Tracy added another plank to their platform,

"Let us stop talking about Right and Left… we need a national conversation about Right and Wrong. Right and Wrong!"

The crowd howled their approval.

Ronny asked, “What does Common Sense say about a politician hiring a hit-man Coyote to kill his competition?”

The response was, "Put him in jail! Put him in jail!" Ronny shook his fists in the air.

As the members of the team who enjoyed heroifying stunts, me, Slick, Hank, Ronny and Goldenboy, created a “Get Even with that Coyote Squad.” We met in the evening at the hotel to plan our strike-back.

Joe Bide-one had been banished from England for sniffing women’s hair while running for Lord Mayor of London. Consequently, he bumped Kamilea out of her acting president job and took over the White House. Joe was looking for someone to strike with a cruise missile to consolidate his power. Through a subtle CIA/FBI/Secret Service connection… Tracy (who had been a journalist) revealed Wilie Coyote to be a nefarious arms-smuggler, assassin, foul-smelling, mangy coyote with roots in the desert. The malodorous coyote was known to be threatifying an endangered bird species… the roadrunner. Those details, plus poor dental hygiene, qualified Wilie for the Presidential Cruise Missile Hit List… (an Obama innovation).

Wilie (god rest his soul) was evaporified at 8 AM the next morning by a cruise missile on the front steps of the Rump Hotel (now Waldorf Astoria) when he resumed his terroristic activity.

President Joe Bide-one was overheard saying, "That's why ya don't fuck with old Joe."

The only collateral damage was a hot dog vendor's cart and seven pigeons. The Rod-Santa team toasted his demise at lunch. Mickey said,

"Gotcha Sucker!" and slugged down his Mountain Dew.

Mini said, "Die, ya mangy bugger."

Those kids were a quick study. We were free to pursue politics as usual again. The bus needed some work. The next few rally's were excellent.

Back home in Pennsylvania, Goldenboy was keen to launch another science project. As East Coast Champions we were eligible for the World Sinus Fair Championship to be held in Maui, Hawaii during the school March Break.

Goldenboy was pumped, "Felix, we are going to build a real rocket and put you into low earth orbit. Dr. Hauptnaud has agreed to support my research and loan us his technician. NASA will grant us up to $100,000 for costs and promises us a summer 'Rocketry Internship'… if we can successfully launch and retrieve a rocket." I have a call in for Elong Mask to see if he will help us get you into low earth orbit. I was briefly speechless.

Goldenboy continued, "For low earth orbit we need to launch at 17,500 mile per hour. Orbiting the Earth every 90 minutes we will fly with the communication satellites and the International Space Station. We would orbit about 1000 miles above the Earth's surface."

"Unlike Laika, the Russian dog who was a stray off the streets of Moscow, and was sent to space in 1957 with one meal and a seven day oxygen supply… you, Felix would return to Earth safely. I think I can get Space-X to give us a small rocket in return for the good PR. Elong Mask cannot resist promotion. Can you imagine, "The Golden Go-nads become Extra-Terrestial!"

I groaned and fondled my precious boys.

"Felix, you would be the first cat in space."

I stammered, using Speechify, "Elong Mask yes. Professor Hauptnaud… no way!"

One dose of Haupnaudification was plenty. An astrocat had to set boundaries.

The BPFP Party did not want to peak too soon… Opa had given us a fabulous kick-off. Afrodite excelled at building a national team… she and Scottie enjoyed weekends at fancy spas and hotels around the country establishing an infrastructure of regional officers and willing volunteers. Online, the BPFP party was huge. We had 60 million pledged members within 2 months of the launch. It was a groundswell of political momentum… The two leaders responded. Ronny got mellow, friendly, funny and open-minded. Tracy grew a serious spine and could emasculate any interviewer with a look, asking, "Now, what does Common Sense say?"

Elong Mask invited me and Goldenboy down to the Space-X launch site in Florida. We stayed overnight with Tracy and Ron in Tallahassee and Elong sent us a helicopter to travel down to the Space-X Launch Site at Cape Canaveral near Orlando.

Elong, supersmart and nerdy, immediately bonded with both Goldenboy and me. We met in his SpaceX executive office, Surrounded by computers, drawings and rocket models.

Art from his 9 children plastered one wall… also mostly rockets. Elong scratched his head, "So, what is your payload?"

Goldenboy pointed at me, "Him, Felix… that's him… 12 pounds of brains and balls. He is completely literafied and Googlified."

Goldenboy hooked up Speechify and my styluses. I told Elong a few Jokes in the Morgan Freedom voice,

"My grandfather was the inventor of the cold air balloon… never really took off." Elong grinned.

"Karl Marx had a sister called Onya… She invented the starting pistol." Elong chuckled.

He said, "Tell you what, Felix… I would love to put the first Tomcat into space…We have room on our next Space-X shuttle in 3 weeks. We will lift him into low earth orbit in a small capsule with a rocket to allow re-entry after a week in orbit."

Goldenboy said, "Wow… really! Can he splash down off the coast of Mauii?"

Elong said, " As long as he wears Space-X gear and his rocket is plastered with our logos. We need the good PR right now… another Tesla caught fire. This is the Tomcat with the famous junk… right? The Pope blessed his balls… Sir Gigi…Right?" He laughed heartily.

He finished, "We will need two weeks to train him. But, Goldenboy, we can give you college credits in Physics and Aeronautics, if you join him."

We moved into the SpaceX training facility.

Chapter 20

The First Catronaut

"A human being or a cat is part of the whole, called by us the "Universe," a part limited by time and space. He (she) experiences life, thoughts and feelings as something separate from the rest, a kind of optical illusion of consciousness. The delusion becomes a kind of prison for us, restricting us to our personal desires and to affection for a few persons nearest to us. Our task must be to free ourselves from this prison by widening our circle of compassion to embrace all living creatures and the whole of nature in its beauty."—Albert Einstein

Goldenboy sat in on college classes in aeronautics and rocket Engineering with University of Central Florida senior students. I was jogging and climbing rope and doing push-ups. Not my idea of fun. My trainers took me to the Greyhound Race Track and I had to chase the mechanical rabbit round and round the oval. One day they let two big greyhounds onto the track behind me to speed me up! I ran like crazy and lost a piece of tail before I leaped over the 10-foot track barrier to lose those mutts. Geeesh!

They filmed my workouts for Elong… Failure was not in Elong's vocabulary. Failure to return from space was not a viable option for this tomcat!

I was on a high protein high cholesterol diet… loads of fish, bacon and cream and supplemental vitamins in the shape of little fish… quite yummy. The scientists and engineers and other space travellers-in-training loved us. Goldenboy and me got a day at Disneyworld and a day at Epcot with priority (no wait) tickets. Disney was leaning toward a movie based on the 'Nine Lives of Felix the Tomcat' book, so we were invited in to meet the CEO and Mickey Mouse for a chat. The Paparazzi did not want to spend $100 to chase us around all day... Me and Goldenboy had a wonderful day at each of the Parks. The rides were great.

During the first week of training, the physiologist doctors started to train me for rapid acceleration and weightlessness. The G force at take-off in the Space-X shuttle would be 3 Gs… 3 times the regular force of gravity… about the same as my volcano ride. The simulator was pretty tame… no Hank's shaky fingers on the buttons. I did not love zero gravity in the flight simulator. At first, I puked a lot and felt dizzy… but by week two my brain had adjustified. The crew gave me my catronaut handle, "Captain Spaceballs."

The week before launch I got to train inside my rocket/capsule which became an attachment to the Space-X Falcon9 two-stage rocket/ Dragon Spacecraft . Space-X has an impressified history of successful launches and landings (189 out of 191). Their rockets service the astronauts of the International Space station. Eat your heart out Dr. Hermann Hauptsnaud. I gave the engineers and scientists 10 minutes of standup every morning via Speechify. I spent a lot of time gathering good jokes to tell during my flight in space. The world would be listening. Me and Goldenboy and Elong had a press conference two days before take-off. The world finally saw my handsome face and my penetrating green eyes. I made National Enquirer's list of the 10 most eligabilized bachelors (in spite of at least 100 Felix Juniors out there in the trailer parks of Pennsylvania). I rankified #3, ahead of Leonardo Decaprio and Pope Benny.

Elong said, "During the flight, I want you on Twitter constantly and I want jokes and quips and play-by-play... we have never had a really funny astronaut. With names like Buzz and Rip and Gus and Sally Ride you would expect a few laughs... but no... macho to the core. Make us laugh, Felix." Goldenboy gave me a thumbs up. Funny I could be.

The engineers taught me how to move about in my tiny capsule... about the size of an average refrigerate... and full of gear. I had a reinforced window to observe space. I would be expected to communicate my findings and feelings and jokes via Speechify. I chose the Morgan Freedom voice. It had gravitas. The engineers loved Speechify. I tested the system in Morgan's voice,

> *"This is God talking. Who the hell sent a tomcat up here? Probably the Yanks... assholes!"*

Elong quipped, "P.G. Felix. P.G!"

Purina Cat Chow offered me a $300,000 a year contract to talk about the Purina Dry Chicken and Fish Cat Chow with Hairball Control. An errantified hairball in space could be a disaster if it lodged in a fan or a motor. Feeling anxious the night before the launch, I took a few hits of catnip to relax.

Scheduled for 9 AM, the launch preparation moved forward like clockwork. Me and Goldenboy rode the elevator up to the hatch to enter my capsule. The rest of the Payload was supplies for the International space Station and a few communication satellites. My space shot was the real deal... not the "Tourist Ride" that Elong sold to billionaires (up to the Space Station... short stay... back down) for $55 million (triple occupancy, meals and space suit included.)

The engineers strapped me into my padded seat and secured all my harnesses. Goldenboy gave me a hug and said, "Love you, Felix." 10,9,8,7,6,5,4,3,2,1... BLASTOFF!

3.5 Gs of Gravity pinned me to my seat… I admit, I did pee a bit. The world flew past my window as I was flung toward heaven. I made my first communication to the world via Speechify, Morgan's bass voice boomed, "Holy shit, Batman!" Those words echoed around the world and became the new 'woke' greeting of Generation Z members everywhere. (I am a Z.)

The trip… at 17,500 miles an hour took us 1000 miles upward in eight and one-half minutes. At that point the Dragon Spacecraft approached the International Space Station and ejectified the FC (Felix Capsule) and a few satellites for independent orbital flight.

I started to transmit my feelings via Speechify, as Morgan Freedom, "Hi Earth, this is God… time to clean up your act and take care of that beautiful shimmering blue and white and green paradise below me. Use it or lose it!"

Apparently, everyone on earth picked up their Big Mac wrappers that day! I gave the world a few jokes,

"Did you hear my extra-terrestrial girlfriend dumped me? Now she is my Space-X."

Morgan chuckled in a booming voice.

"Space-X is planning to send 10 cows into space next year. It will be the herd shot around the World."

Morgan laughed. *"Why haven't aliens visited our solar system? It only got a 'One Star review'."*

Morgan added, "Bada Bing, Bada Boom.!"

Space flight was easy. It was like sitting at a computer watching great scenery. I could see Earth below, out the window. We circled the entire Earth every 90 minutes. Earth's surface is 71% water... so the whole place looked like a giant blue marble. I had a few experiments to carry out... mostly testing my intelligence and reflexes in zero gravity. Zero gravity was fun. If you farted, you were propelled across the capsule... and you had to smell it for forty minutes. I was glad that Slick was not along. (he had terrible gas.)

I sent greeting to all my friends and made a few 'Rump' jokes. I threw 'Common Sense' into almost every sentence. Opa interviewed me,

Opa: "Felix, what quality would you say made you the first Tomcat in space?"

Me: "Common Sense got me here and Common Sense will get me home." (Truthfully, it was my inability to say "No" to Goldenboy!)

Opa: "Felix, what will you do next? Knighted by the Pope, Stand-up comedy in Vegas, a motorcycle over the Grand Canyon... now a space flight. What comes next for the world's most spectacular cat?"

Me: "Common sense" says lunch! I got some delicious Purina Dry Chicken Cat Chow with Hairball Control waitin for this cat to enjoy. Yum!" Ka-ching... the royalties were rolling in from Purina.

Opa: "Felix... we will talk again on the day you splash down in the Pacific near Mauii. Be safe! Respect!"

The flight was wonderful... the stars and the galaxies were crisp and clear to see outside the Earth's atmosphere. The Earth was a pristine, beautiful globe... occasionally comets shot through the sky. Two hundred billion galaxies spun around me in my tiny space capsule. The silence was deafening! Every once in a while my capsule's mini-rocket motor would rumble to life to correctify my orbit... or avoid a piece of lethal space junk. There are 30,000 pieces up there, some as small as a dime, moving at 20,000 miles per hour... beware!

I chatted daily with Goldenboy, Scottie, Gloomer and Afrodite. Me and Slick had a few rich conversations in Catonese which was finally recognized by humans as real speech. I spoke to the President of China, Xi Jinping, and his cat, JinPong (in catonese). JinPong was a snotty asshole (a Siamese)... arrogant and entitlified, in my humblified opinion.

Space-X was selling Felix in Space mugs and hats and T-shirts like crazy. I signed to do a Tesla commercial... where the AI automatic steering veers the slick roadster away from flattening me into a grease spot on the highway of life. Goldenboy had enough $ in his college fund to take 6 PhDs. My major charity, "Cats against Castration" was brimming with funds. Pope Benny was on our Board of Directors and, in Rome, 50 cardinals had formed a choir to sing "Every Sperm is Sacred" at our Annual General Meeting in Miami in May. Most of the cardinals wanted a holiday somewhere warm. They had lost interest in sperm during their 30s. I, personally, had no interest in sperm, but I loved sex.

My week in space was amazing. The Hubble Space Telescope (1992) and now, the Webb Space Telescope (2022—100 times more powerful) have allowed astronomers to look much further out into the universe (back in time). The number of identified galaxies in the universe has climbed from 20 billion in the 1980s to 200 billion with Hubble and now up to 2 trillion with the Webb Telescope. (1 trillion=1000 billion).

Each galaxy has at least 200 billion stars, The stars in the universe are at least 200 sextillions in number. That is a huge number… 200,000,000,000,000,000,000,000 stars! Our universe is 13.5 billion years old and expanding faster than the speed of light. Looking at stars and galaxies and Earth humbled me… I was awed by the beauty and the power of nature.

As promised, Opa called on the morning of splashdown near Hawaii. She was bubbly,

Opa: "So Felix, how has space travel changed my favourite Tomcat?"

Me: "Opa, I am awed by the massive scale and beauty of the universe. The Earth is a gem... we must nourish and protect it. Life is precious."

Opa: "Wow, Felix... your words are profound. Would you go again?"

Me: "As long as I land safely today... yes, I would go back to space in a heartbeat! The coolest experience of my short life!"

To push me out of Low Earth Orbit back toward Earth the SpaceX engineers burned my rocket engine to drive me within 60 miles of the Earth's surface, where the atmosphere began. From 60 miles in my capsule would pass through increasingly dense atmosphere that was spinning with the Earth. Ceramic and carbon fibre panels on the surface of my spacecraft shielded me from the intense heat created by re-entry. I was comfortable inside the craft but would have been a flambeed Tomcat outside. Air friction and the rocket motor slowed my descent and at 10,000 feet my parachutes... one at first... then 3 more larger ones deployed to drop me towards earth gently. My rocket journey took me 2 million miles... around earth 63 times.

When I looked down to spot Mauii... all I could see was a massive, gaping caldera of a massive mother-fucking active volcano below me. I was over the center of the Big Island of Hawaii. Smoke and steam were rising all around me I could smell sulfur. Basalt boulders as big as stoves were being chucked skyward by the angry eruption. Molten rock lava glowed and spattered hundreds of feet into the air beneath me.

I was directly over Mauna Kea… the biggest active volcano in the world… which happened to be erupting. The open mouth atop the volcano (caldera) measured 3 miles by 2 miles with 600 foot walls down to a pit of bubbling, boiling, liquid red lava. My styluses flew over the keyboard and Morgan Freedom growled…

"Looks like we are landing on the biggest fucking active volcano in the world! Is that the plan?"

I was sweating bullets and shaking with fear. SpaceX responded, "Relax, Captain Spaceballs, relax Captain Spaceballs. We got this."

I felt the engine rumbling, pushing my craft South-West. The engineer said, "O.K. Captain Spaceballs… you have a 25 mph Tradewind blowing you South-West at 8000 feet. You will hit the ocean 2 miles offshore near Captain Cook. (The intrepid Brit who stumbled across Hawaii, New Zealand and other popular vacation spots.)"

Captain Cook bit the dust near my splash down spot… he was scrapping with a Hawaiian chief over a row boat and got stabbed. We skirted over the southeast rim of the caldera and flew down over the lava-coated mountainside of Mauna Kea.

Splash! The ocean. I bobbed in the waves for a while, yelling, via Speechify.

"Yahoo! Yeah! We did it!"

Within 20 minutes, a SpaceX helicopter picked my capsule and we flew ashore. My legs were wobbly and weak. It felt great to have a wilder-pee in the bushes again. The first catronaut was home.

Chapter 21

Maui and the World Science Fair

"The saddest aspect of life right now is that science gathers knowledge faster than society accumulates wisdom."—Isaac Asimov

I joined Goldenboy in Maui later in the day. The World Middle School Science Fair contest for the top 30 young scientists was in progress.

I crashed at the guest house after a big feed of fresh cream, bacon and fresh Mahi-mahi fish. I slept soundly for 16 hours. Goldenboy, ecstatified by our space success, was full of beans. He gave me hugs.

The exhibits were set up at the University of Hawaii campus in Kahului, Maui. Because my space flight involved SpaceX and NASA it did not qualify for the science fair… but Elong had agreed to be the guest speaker via Zoom for the awards banquet on the second evening of the show. Goldenboy set up a visual display of all our data from the Harvard experiment (Nine Lives) and we played a short movie of the ultimate explosion of our Volcano (Mount Stromboli) and the inundation of the judges (Dr. SLUT and Dr. Nuts) and Harvard alumni in gunky, red, fake lava. Dr. SLUT was on long term disability with PTSFD (Post Traumatic Fucking Stress Disorder) and catatonia. Dr. Nuts was a judge at the Maui gathering, but hid in the shrubs every time she saw me. She was twitching and repeating "Son of a bitch!" every 10 seconds… Tourette's!

The projects presented at the gathering were amazing and innovative. Some of my favorites were:

1. A natural rubber sap coagulant made from natural Bilimbi tree fruit to replace toxic, expensive formic acid.

2. Use of Rhizobian bacteria in accelerating crop germination in adverse weather with reduced fertilizer use. Over 120,000 measurements in the data set. An aid to world hunger.

3. Ethanol production from waste products (garbage dumps). "Your garbage is my martini."

4. Improving hearing loss with tactile sound recognition.

5. A low-cost paper-based water filter synthesized from wild grasses (wipe your ass with grass).

Me and Goldenboy spend the two days wandering around chatting and learning from the participants.

The banquet was sponsored by SpaceX at the Bistro Casanova in Kahului. All 30 of the young geniuses attended... without parents... it was a loud and boisterous affair.

They served a huge salad bar plus a variety of pasta dishes, pizzas and Lasagnas, plus 5 flavors of gelato. A buttered-bun fight broke out between the North American and European contingents.

Goldenboy, who was introducing Elong, shoved me up to the mike to do some standup to prevent the bun-fight from going nuclear. I did the pre-recorded lip-sink Speechify routine .... so I could do some slapstick to add to the jokes.

"Did you hear the one about Will, the Newfoundland lobster fisherman who lost his wife while she was fishing on the shoreline.

His two friends approached him at his boat in the harbour.

"Will, me boy. We got some bad news, some good news and some great news for ye!"

Will said, "Tell me the bad news first."

His friend Davie said, "We found your wife. She was drowned and is on the bottom of the cove."

Will said, "What about the good news?"

Davie said, "The good news is that 6 lobsters were feedin' on her..." Davie handed 2 massive lobsters over to Will.

Will said, "Well, what's the great news, then?"

Davie said, "We think there will be at least a dozen lobsters when we pull her back up tomorrow."

I continued, "To get you guys to stop shelling each other with buttered buns... I am going to give you a few Einstein quotes... he was the Elong Mask of the 20th century."

Einstein said, *"There are only two ways to live your life. You can live as if nothing is a miracle or you can live as if everything is a miracle."*

Einstein also said, *"My only genius talent is inquisitiveness."*

Finally, he said, *"To be free means to be independent, not influenced by what others think and say."*

Goldenboy took over the microphone, "Hi, fellow young scientists. It has been so much fun to meet you and see your projects here in this tropical paradise. Your projects were brilliant and I commend you on your originalty and your passion. I am so lucky to have a brilliant, funny, Gogglified Tomcat in my life... Thanks, Felix."

I bowed as the paediatric geniuses hooted and clapped. A few buns were thrown.

Elong Mask's face suddenly appeared via Zoom on a giant screen in the dining room.

Goldenboy continued, "I want to introduce an amazing human being. Not only does he lead 5 dynamic companies including SpaceX, Tesla and Twitter, he also has 9 children! And... he makes time to talk to and help a 13 year old boy from Pennsylvania who wants to put a tomcat into Low Earth Orbit. Young scientists of the world, meet Elong Mask via Zoom.

Elong began, "Congratulations, young scientists. The fact that you are sitting eating pizza and throwing buns in Mauii means three things about you are true:"

> "One: You were born with the precious gift of an inquisitive, hungry brain that searches for truth and knowledge. Never stop that search. Do not let anyone or anything stop you.
>
> Two: You were gifted with a support network of teachers and parents and friends and role models. Relationships need work. Nourish your network. Say

thank you and recognize those who help you. Help others.

Three: Be tenacious. Never give up. Chase your dreams."

He continued, "I will give you an example. Goldenboy, who I love, approached me… out of the blue… and said… "I want to put my Tomcat, Felix into low Earth orbit. My cat has a hyperthymesified memory, he is completely Googlified and he can communicate at 400 words a minute in 17 languages via 'Speechify'."

Elong chuckled, "An outrageous project… that I could not possibly refuse. Three days ago Felix returned from a 2 million mile trip, circling around Earth 63 times in one of our SpaceX rockets. "

He wrapped it up, "So, young geniuses… Think outside the box… and never, ever stop."

Me and Goldenboy did some hiking and took a few tours around the island. I was the only cat. I did some solo mousing and ratting one night, but I missed my pal Slick. Not a horny Queen was located!

It felt great to return home to the manshun in Fox Chapel Hills. The entire family, including Rosa and Scottie were thrilled to see us back. I set up speechify to answer all the questions about space in my Morgan Freedom voice.

Rosa asked, "Did you see heaven?"

Morgan replied, "Yes, but it was cloudy and Jesus was on holiday. But God and I worked on our voices together."

Rosa said, "Gato sabeltoto!" "Smartassed cat" (Rosettas stones).

Gloomer was fascinated to see all the photos of earth from the hundreds taken by SpaceX. We mounted our wall plaque from Elong that read "First Cat in Space. A Pioneer. Felix the Tomcat".

Magazine and internet articles abounded about my historic flight and about the amazing 13 year boy behind my success. Elong described it as a "Goodwill Bonanza" for him and SpaceX. They planned to name the next Tesla model 'Model Felix.'

Scottie and Afrodite planned to capitalize our adventure in political ads for the Common Sense (BPFP) Party campaign. Rosa made us a wonderful supper of Fajitas and beans and rice and we had a lively discussion. V-Domes absence was a step toward happiness for all his family. I agreed to meet up with Slick after dark. (I messaged him through Hank).

It was a beautiful, moonlit, late-March night with a foot of packed snow on the ground. Slick was in the crotch of the maple… whistling. "Memories" from "Cats" evoked many scenes.

He said, "How are they hangin, kid?"

I said, "East-West and ready for action. No horny Queens in space."

Slick had many questions about space and Hawaii and we chatted for a long time, catching up. Slick reported that Hank's brother-in-law, Mike, the 'furry' Beagle, also known as 'Yoda,' had moved in with them... but was living in a heated doghouse under the trailer. Freeda had gave him an ultimatum... "Lose the Beagle or lose me!" and he had said, "Woof, woof!", possibly condemning himself to a life of gobblifying dog chow!

Slick loved the drama, saying, "What a fucking psycho."

We headed over to the old barn and granary to dine on mice and rattus rattus... quite delicious. We tag teamed on barn swallows... yummy, in spite of the feathers.

Slick reported, "Kid, we are seriously behind on the horny Queen front."

We got to work and shouldered our burden. Yoda was making a nuisance of himself, howling at the moon, and chasing his own tail. What a loser.

After using up our full quota of swimmers, Me and Slick collapsed on the roof of the trailer to rest. We were drifting off to sleep when we heard, "Leave me alone! You giant fucking cat!" from Yoda down below.

As we looked down we were attacked from behind by a giant cat… It was a bobcat (Lynx Rufus…Google).

This Bobcat was 4 feet long, 2 feet high and sported 50 pounds of muscle and teeth. His coat was beautiful…much like mine, with rosettified brown, black white and pale orange spots and swirls. It had tuftified big ears and a nasty attitude. He was super stealthy.

His massive jaws were clamped across the back of Slick's neck. Realizing that Slick was about to become a continental breakfast, I attacked the bobcat. I bit him in the head and scratched at his eyes with my front claws and shrieked my most feral scream. He let go of Slick and turned his charm on me. That Bobcat was Felixicidal!

He quickly sunk his choppers into my abdomen and shook me till I briefly fainted. Then he grabbed me by the neck and kept shaking me. I was toast.

A huge explosion interrupted the night! I was released … free! I thought… 'Crap! Not heaven again!'

My saviour this time was Hank, who stood in his pajamas on top of the Amazon Van with a smoking shotgun. Yoda was hiding in the truck, whimpering. Me and Slick were badly shaken and somewhat lightly eaten.

Slick said, "That was a fucking bobcat! Nasty as hell."

I agreed, "Wow! That is another life gone, Slick... We are down to 4 ½ lives again." We had aged to middle-age (from 7 lives to 4 ½) again in 4 months. But we were still alive.

We both shot Hank 'high fives' with our paws.

We went inside the trailer for some cream and balony and tuna. Yoda took off his furry suit and put on jeans and a sweatshirt and ate a salami sandwich and drank a beer. Hank just shook his head. Yoda (Mike) said, "Life in the wild, as a Beagle, sucks. I wonder about being a Doberman? Freeda likes Dobermans." Mike was an open-minded guy.

Hank gave me a lift home in the morning... both Me and Slick were rattled and hurting. That bobcat had nasty choppers and strong jaws. I went into the manshun for some cream and tuna and a big sleep. Goldenboy put antibiotic cream on my bite marks and punctures. Me and Slick restified ourselves for a few days before getting back to our nightly roundezvous.

We had another road trip planned... to Miami for the Annual Generalized Meeting of my charity, "Cats Against Castration". Slick and Hank were going to join me and Goldenboy and Gloomer. Our meeting would co-incidify with a Common Sense Party rally, also in Miami.

Chapter 22

On the Road Once Again... Miami ... "Gateway to Latin America"

"Whenever trouble arises and things look bad, there is always one Individual who perceives a solution and is willing to take command. Very often, that individual is crazy."—Dave Barry

We took off on a Friday afternoon after school to drive to Florida in the big Caddy that V-Dome left in the manshun's garage. The "Cats Against Castration" annual General Meeting was scheduled for the Wednesday- Thursday. We planned to visit Charleston, South Carolina and Savannah, Georgia and Saint Augustine, Florida to have a history lesson on the way south. Gloomer's research for an essay on 'Slavery in the South' would be enriched by visiting major slave ports and trading centers along the way.

At the last moment, Scottie asked to join us on the trip. He functioned well as a surrogate father for Gloomer and GB (Golden boy had shortened his handle). Scottie loved hanging with his 'Step-kids.' As an expert pilot, Hank muscled the Caddy all the way to Roanoke, Virginia before we stopped for the night. Scottie and Gloomer played great tunes on guitar and banjo and all 6 of us sang and howled together,

"On the road again,

Like a band of gypsies we go down the highway

We're the best of friends

Insisting that the world keep turning our way

And our way

Is on the road again." (Willie Nelson)

In Roanoke, we stopped at an OK Motel and crashed in a large room. Me and Slick did some mousing and ratting and a pinch of Queening… there was a nearby trailer park. We took off after being chased by 3 slow, but tuff, Tomcats and a three-legged pit-bull. We had no extra lives to spend!

Saturday morning we grabbed a scrumptious breakfast at a Waffle House (good bacon and sausage and milk) and hit the road in the Caddy. GB, Gloomer, and Hank and Scottie played the question game. Scottie asked hard political questions:

Scottie Q: "Can the Common Sense Party win the election in 2024 with Tracy and Ronny?"

A (Hank): "If they beat the Democrats and Republicans, yes! Will they? Maybe… Yeah, maybe."

A (Goldenboy… GB): "Yes, I think the US is ready for a government that works and serves the people. Rump's support is dying. Joe is not popular with the Democrats and they have no-one else even remotely interesting. The US is ready for a dynamic third-party government."

A (Gloomer): "Tracy and Ronny are perfect. Absolutely… we can win. We are beyond ready for a charismatic, young woman President. Tracy is a wonderful candidate… smart, left-leaning but family- centered. People love her. And Ronny will bring along many Republicans… he has a brain and a track record of good leadership as Governor in Florida (unlike Rump)."

GB asked Scottie a question: "How many Democrat and Republican members of the House and the Senate will switch to the BPFP Party?

Scottie replied, "As you know, GB, they are allowed to switch parties at will. So far, we have interest expressed by 165 of 435 from the House and 42 of 100

Senators. But, they are politicians… so, who knows? Also, at least 200 new candidates, who love our platform, have expressed interest in running with the Common Sense Party. Afrodite and I are pumped about the next year. We have a Party Meeting and retreat for our new party scheduled next Friday- Saturday at the Intercontinental Hotel. We have 1200 registrants including our "Billionaire Club" who get to pay for conventions and costs … but get no say in the Party Platform. We are listening to the Common folk… like us!

Q: (Gloomer): Scottie… what is the Common Sense Party position on abortion.

A (Scottie): Common Sense would answer… who is the pregnant person? Who will raise the child? Common Sense says that the pregnant individual should have that choice. Not some judge or politician. Are we ready for Common Sense? We will find out. Gloomer nodded and gave Scottie a high five.

Q (Hank): The Electoral College… isn't it time for that to go?

A (Scottie): absolutely, Hank. That was established in the 1770s so that the few chosen literate people from the 13 colonies could travel Philadelphia to elect the next president. With technology and education, the system is both unfair and subject to corruption. The popular vote should choose the president. We wonder about making the second most-popular candidate the

Vice-President… but the egos might clash. We admire Lincoln's concept of "a Team of Rivals".

Between the great discussion and a few burger stops and a serious snooze, the trip down to Charleston flew by. Goldenboy hooked up my Speechify and I entertained the crew with about 30 jokes, which they loved.

"What is the difference between a northern fairy tale and a southern fairy tale?"

Answer: "A Northern fairy tale starts with, "Once Upon a Time, and a southern tale starts with, "Y'all ain't gonna believe this…"

I gave them another:

"A poor woman from Georgia loses her husband of 50 years. When she calls the local paper to write an obituary she is told.

The fee is $1 a word.

She replies, "OK. Here it is… "Billy Bob died."

The editor says, "Minimum 7 word obituary, sorry Ma'am."

She replies," Write "Billy Bob died. 1983 Ford pick-up cheap."

And yada, yada, yada…

We drove through the slums of Charleston, South Carolina and found a small hotel near the waterfront. We found a local restaurant that allowed cats. Me and Slick had fresh sea bass and chicken gizzards with a big bowl of cream. The humans dined on Southern specials… fried chicken, ham biscuits , sweet iced tea and Hush Puppies with pecan pie. Me and Slick enjoyed some vanilla ice cream.

We were up early to walk around downtown Charleston which was founded in 1670 as a natural sheltered harbour by the British. In spite of an earthquake, a fire, smallpox, yellow fever and malaria…the settlers hung on. 400,000 African slaves and 40,00 local aboriginals were eventually sold to owners at the slave auction in Charleston between 1700 and 1875. Children and fathers and mothers were often separated and sold to different owners… sometimes hundreds of miles apart.

The slave trade made the city the most affluent community in the 13 Colonies. The stately mansions along the harbour wall attestified to the money gained from slavery. We walked through the slave market museum and along the harbor wall. Fort Sumpter, where the Union Ships first fired on the Confederacy (over slavery) in 1861 sat offshore in the harbor. Ultimately 620,000 Americans died in the Civil War.

Sobered by our first real look at slavery, we were all happy to have Scottie give us a history lesson on the Southern economy of the 1700s and 1800s, which depended entirely on "Free slave labor" to generate enormous riches. From tobacco, cotton, and indigo to sugar, all of the Southern crops required brutal labor in the hot sun.

After lunch, we took off for Savannah, Georgia, another fascinating coastal city at the mouth of the Savannah River, established in 1751. The city has many beautiful southern mansions built around 22 downtown parks full of huge Southern live oaks covered with Spanish moss. It was the port for exporting Georgias huge cotton and indigo crops to Europe, again dependent on slave labor.

We finished the day in Saint Augustine, possibly discovered by Juan Ponce de Leon, a Spaniard, in 1513. Ponce was searching for the legendary island, Bimini, which was believed to be the site of the Fountain of Youth. He became the first Spanish Governor of Florida. De Leon bit the dust several years later from being shot in the thigh with a poisoned arrow by a disgruntled native brave. St. Augustine featured incredible Spanish colonial architecture dating back 500 years. The Spanish built a huge fort…Castillo de San Marcos…in 1695 and hung on to Florida for 200 years. They protected the town and their sugar, citrus, rice and sugar crops… from the Indigenous tribes and French and English marauders.

That night, Me and Slick went hunting among orange groves and sugar cane fields. We met lots of rodents but also poisonous snakes, the Cottonmouth and the Eastern Diamondback rattlesnake. Me and Slim were on our best behavior after that Bobcatty thingy.

We arrived in Miami on Tues evening, ready for our "Cats against Castration" annual General meeting and convention. We held the event at the AC Hotel Marriot Miami Beach- which had meeting rooms, a beach and good quality accommodation.

Apart from the 40 'Cardinal Choir' and GB and me, Hank and Slick, we had no idea who might show up. We had a list of 600 donors, including Pope Benny who was going to 'Zoom' into the Wednesday evening supper meeting. Gloomer and Scottie got dropped off at the Intercontinental to meet Afrodite and the Common Sense Political team.

The registrants for the 'C against C' meeting belonged to four groups:

One: Insane cat ladies who had at least three cats in their hand luggage and wore Cat-Themified apparel. They looked like a lot of fun.

Two: Pudgy singing Cardinals from Rome who wore bad golf outfits and hummed loudly to demonstrate their purrfect pitch.

Three: a whole chapter of the New York City Gay Cat Furries Drama Ensemble … 165 of them. The group, in full fursona, were gorgeous and were staging an impromptu version of the Musical, "Cats" by the swimming pool. It was riveting.

Golden Boy immediately signed the Cat Furries up for 'Entertainment' after the banquets on Wednesday and Thursday. Each of the cat furries had at least three different 'catsuit' outfits. Their grooming was impeccified.

> Four: The fourth group were 6 serious, Latino-looking fellas with Goatees and stubble wearing Leisure suits in bright pastel colors with multiple bulges in their jackets with matching ball caps that read " Equiopo de Recuperacion de Reliqias Religiosas Cubanas." I assumed they were monks or friars or some other brand of religious whackos.

Editors Note: Felix, can you write about anything other than a Tomcat's genitals. This is not "100 Shades of Grey."

Felix Note: Great Title Idea. You are fired... again.

Chapter 23

The Cats Against Castration Annual General Meeting

"The meeting is over, but people keep asking dumb questions."—Anon

The Annual General Meeting started at 6 pm sharp in the banquet room of the hotel. Most of the 241 registrants showed up... including the cat ladies and the entire New York City Gay Cat Furries Ensemble and the 6 swarthy guys who badly needed a shave. The stubblified men stuck together and were muttering in Spanish and pointing at me!

Cardinal Dinardo, our good friend from the Italian tour, gave a lengthy, but moving, blessing on the topics of good food, genitals and cats, and we all dug in. Some of the Cat Furries were pretty feisty (New

York…Aye!) … wanting both human bean food… Chick-en-a-la- King Latino with veggies, salad and buttered buns… PLUS a saucer of cream , PLUS bacon and sausage and BOTH champagne and wine… Slim had to go down and bite a few of the most entitled Cat Furries. Cardinal Dinardo warned, "The word is some Cats are piggin' out at this banquet… you will get unpleasantly fat!"

No buns were thrown except by Goldenboy who was at that age! The cat ladies brought their cats, who were walking around, hopping from table to table, stealing the Furries' cream whenever the Furries put their cat heads on. Furries (of all breeds and species) cannot buy life insurance. Fursona heads block vision. The rate of death per 1000 Furries is 3 per 100 outings while in full Fursona. Three of the York City Gay Cat Furry Acting Ensemble were already in the ICU in Miami. One got hit by a cement truck!

Pope Benny graciously joined us by 'Zoom' and gave an inspiring speech on sperm, genitals and the Free Cats of Rome. Benny loved cats. He finished with, "I zend my special auf wiederzein to my darlink cat friend, Felix, Ze First Knight of Ze Order of Ze Golden Sperm. Sir Gigi, you have ze varmist place in my heart. God bless you and zos Golden Boyzz."

The Gay Cat Furries Drama Ensemble of New York gave a stirring performance of 'Cats' complete with exquisified dancing and a small orchestra.

'Old Deuterostomy', the geriatric cat, actually had a heart attack while ascendifying to the 'Heavierside Layer'. Hank, who was at the head table with me, GB, Slick and Cardinal Dinardo and a few crazy cat ladies, grabbed a defibrillator and saved Old Deuterostomy's life. Old Deutero was plenty pissed because Hank burned a hole through his best 'Old Cat Outfit.' The show went on with vigor.

The 40 'Singin' Cardinals' did a bang-up job singing "Every Sperm is Sacred' in 12 part harmony. They sang by candlelight, dressed in red robes and Galeros, marching militantly round and round dining room. The 'Gay Cat Furries of New York Drama Ensemble' gave them a rousing standing ovation. Unfortunately, one of the Cardinals and one cat lady caught fire, but Hank put them out with a fire extinguisher.

The Hotel insisted on a $3000 damage deposit for each future function. The Miami Fire Department arrived and called it a "Faulty (almost False) Alarm" since no-one got killed or severely roastified. One of the New York Gay Cat Furries was a lawyer but she kept dropping her business cards… with no opposable thumbs.

It was an inspiring meeting. Pope Benny agreed to stay on the Board of Governors and Cardinal Dinardo became our new elected president. We voted to use $300,000 of our budget to start and fund Free Cat Sanctuaries retreats in the US, Europe and in Latin America.

Cardinal Dinardo and GB and me had a good chat via Speechify after the meeting. He pointed at the 6 swarthy gentlemen in bulgy leisure suits leaving the dining room. He said,

"Felix... do you know who those gangstas are?"

I said, "Weird priests?"

He shook his head, "No, Felix. They are Cuban Catholic Church hit- men. Those six are the notorious members of "the Cuban Religious Relic Recovery Team". They are after your Golden Gonads, Son. The bounty on your blessed, space-travelled, knighted gonads is up to $500,000 in Europe. Bounty-hunters from all over the world are after your boys! They plan to seize them as relics for the Catedral de San Cristobal in Havana.

I gulped, "Oh Shit! Of course... those hats and those bulges!"

Goldenboy and me and Slick and Hank switched to a different hotel room... Hank loaded his Beretta M9 pistol, from his days in the Marine Corp. We agreed to escape to Pennsylvania immediately after the wrap-up lunch meeting (and performance of 'Cats' by the pool) the following day. We chatted by Zoom with Afrodite and Gloomer and Scottie who were at the Intercontinental, ready to start the Common Sense Party retreat and Rally. The hit-man team remained our private concern.

For the first time in months I began to fear for the loss of my gonads... and possibly, the remainder of my lives. Our courageous team made a pinky-paw promise to stick together... no matter what happened.

Editors Note: You are back on that 'TOPIC' again! Felix!

Felix Note: Eat shit! Editor. My book, my topics! You are fired again.

Chapter 24

An Unplanned Adventure

"I knew when I met you that an adventure was going to happen."—Winnie the Pooh

Our charity dinner and wrap up was scheduled to be held outside on the patio dining area overlooking the pool. Our group reconified the area to look for areas where the Cuban 6 might try to ambush me. We were all set, at the head table, when the attendees began to wander in. The 21 cat ladies… with two or three cats on slender leashes… wore baggy dresses, sun-glasses and floral beach hats. They had formed into groups according to the brand or breed of their cats. The Persian and Siamese crowd were drinking Mimosas and the cat-rescue alleycat crew were sluggin Buds. The cats (with gonads) were busy fornicating (where possible) and fighting each other. Every charity has its flaws.

The New York Gay Cat Furry Drama Ensemble arrived in waves, all wearing spanking new cat outfits completely in fursona. Even Old Deuterostomy had a super-sharp, grey-white long-haired cat outfit on. The furries sat in the middle of the banquet area ... all 165 of them. The 6 Cubans with the same outfits for 3 days (B.O. city) observed us from the tropical vegetation separating the dining patio from the pool deck.

Hank, with a Beretta bulge in his light jacket (shoulder holster) sat at the very end of our head table... our enforcer.

Goldenboy, who was the treasurer of the charity, gave a brief financial rundown and presented the budget for the upcoming year. No-one actually cared. The Cubans moved into position with 3 gangstas at tables blocking both exits from the dining patio to the pool deck.

Father Donato said a lengthy grace... involving food, the sunshine, go-nads and cats. The food for lunch was shrimp po boy sandwiches and multiple salads served buffet-style with guacamole and tortilla chips. The 40 Cardinals could not resist another performance of "Every Sperm is Sacred" and even the 6 Cubans sang along, marching around the dining patio.

The entire group then moved chairs over to the edge overlooking the pool deck to watch "Cats, the Thursday Version" by the New York City Gay Cat Furries Drama Ensemble, performed with wild enthusiasm. The Cuban 6 hung on the edge of the crowd.

Of course, Old Deuterostomy had another cardiac arrest on his way to the Heavierside Layer… and Hank, our bodyguard, had to give CPR and defibrillate the old cat again. Another cat suit went up in smoke.

During the disturbance strong hands suddenly grabbed me, and Slick and Goldenboy and stubby gun barrels were pushed into our ribs.

Chapter 25

My Night of Purgatory

"I don't want to brag, but I put the puzzle together in two days and the box said 2-4 years."—Anon

We heard a gruff voice, "Hora dedejar, a cato! Tu gonadas son mis gonadas, Buster!" ("Time to leave, cat! Your go-nads are my go-nads, Buster!" Rosetta's Stones) We were forcefully hauled through the lobby and tossed into a waiting white panel van that said "Gonzales Camion de Flores". ("Gonzales Flower Truck." Rosettas's Stones).

As we travelled I could hear Goldenboy pleading with the chief Cuban thug (in rudimentary Spanish) to release us. Goldenboy repeated Governor Desanta's name… over and over.

Fifteen minutes later the truck with me, Slick, Goldenboy and the 6 Cubans bumped to a stop on a jetty extendifyed into the Atlantic at the very south end of Miami Beach. The Flower van was hidden in a warehouse. A fifty foot grubby, black trawler boat sat at the quay… it's engines rumbling. For some reason, the chief thug, Ricardo, cut Goldenboy's zip ties and released him once dusk descended on harbour. Goldenboy shook his hand and said, "Gracias, Senor." Goldenboy was free.

Me and Slick were manhandled aboard the fishing trawler and confined to small cages with tarps thrown over them. With my primitive Spanish, I could tell that the missionaries, or possibly mercenaries, were having second thoughts about their bold catnapping. However, they passed around some potent weed and settled in for the 92-mile boat trip to Havanna, Cuba.

As we glided across the harbor heading south, the chief Cuban thug/hit man, Ricardo, sang, in a mellow baritone,

"Cada esperma es sagredo.

Cada esperma es genial.

Si se desperdiciaun esperma,

Dios se pone bastante furioso." (Every sperm is sacred… yada, yada..)

The remaining 5 ganstas and the ship crew, wasted with weed, joined in the chorus, marching around the deck. The shores of Florida retreated into the distance behind us…

Locked in my steel cage, lonely and forlorn, I reflected on my life. Who the hell was I? Was I the brilliant, scientific, daring, adventurous, space-traveling, knighted, stud of a Tomcat (Sir GiGi)?

Or, was I a cold, lonely, frightened, angry, mysogynistified, misfit of a Tomcat who was bullied into ridiculous and dangerous adventures by a spoiled, rich, bored guppy-child. It was a tough question that I had avoided for many months.

With shelter and regular food and friendship and love… I had grown and improved. I no longer lashed out in anger attacking my 'owners' and their misguided hair-pieces. I had matured into a confident, stand-up comedian to Popes and professors and possibly, Presidents. I had traveled around the world and through space who had masterfied Speechify and Google … and had rejected Harvard. I was buddies with Elong and Pope Benny. Having masterfied the Tomcat code of survival, my gang of loyal friends supported me.

I realized that my grip on my go-nads had cost me dearly… but it also defined me. All the brilliant little Felixes out there would find a way, like I had, to get by. No, I could not give-upify. Life was a marathon not a sprint.

I could hear Slick moving in his cage nearby. In Cantonese, I reassured him,

"Hey, Slick, Hang in there. We are going to Cuba. We got this!"

Slick was chuckling, "Hell ya, Felix. And I am going to open a string of Burger King franchises."

We cruised all night in the smoky old diesel boat. The thugs took the tarps off our cages at dawn. We soon saw palm trees and heard lots of birds singing and people chatting in Spanish. Pulling into a small harbor, the gangstas tied up the boat and transferred us to a pick- up truck… still in our cages. Ricardo said, "Nosotros vamos a la Habana para ver al arzobispo." (We go to Havanna to see the archbishop. (Rosetta's stones))

It was hard not to fondle my go-nads. (dramatic foreshadowing? ...or not!)

The Cathedral de San Cristobel in Havanna was immense and beautiful and perched on the City harbour wall. It was built by Jesuits after 1750. Archbishop Corteza was the boss-man of Catholicks in Cuba and our arrival had him on his feet, dressed in a white robe, in his office and thoroughly pissed-off at 7 AM on a Friday morning.

The Archbishop glowered at Ricardo, "Pendejo.?Por que secuestraste al nino?" ("Asshole. Why did you kidnap the boy?" (Rosetta's stones))

He added, "Ahora tengo al puto papa en mi culo." ("Now I have the fucking Pope on my tail." (Rosetta's stones.))

Suddenly charming, the aging Archbishop beamed a warm smile at me and Slick, who were sporting flex-cuffs (front and back legs). The bishop yelled in Spanish and Ricardo cut off our cuffs and a harried nun appeared with big bowls of cream, bacon, sausages and little cat-treats. I grinned at Slick and he grinned back. Archbishop Corteza, smiled and said, "Welcome to Cuba. We are privileged to have you visit us."

The archbishop gave us a personal tour of the Cathedral and showed us into a comfy bedroom and said, "Thank you for your visit to Cuba. It is our pleasure to host a famous Tomcat and his friend. The Pope says Ciao."

The Marine helicopter arrived an hour later to fly us back to Miami.

Chapter 26

Back in Miami

"If you think travel is dangerous, try routine, it's routine that is dangerous."—Paula Coehlo

Afrodite and Scottie got me a black and white striped prison suit with a cap to wear for my Stand-up spot at the Common Sense Friday evening at the Intercontinental.

I started with, *"Had to bust out of a Cuban jail to get to this gig... Oh well, at least I got a chance to pack my junk!"*

That one brought down the house. The story of my kidnapping had leaked and gone viral around the world. There was a picture of a grim-faced Ricardo, his gun poking in my ribs, captifying me with little flex-ties on my limbs. He was about to chuck me into a Flower

Van. I looked very handsome and calm. Pictures of my gonads had re-emmerged onto front pages around the world.

I continued my jokes, *"Did you hear that the Archbishop of Cuba felt the catnapping went well?*

"The catholic Church of Cuba had to pay a mere $200,000 ransome to send me back to Miami."

The crowd went wild and I was just getting warmed up.

Felix was back!

THE END

Aurther's Note: Will there be a sequel? Will Felix and his gang strike again? I am just a very smart cat with a hyperthymefied memory … but, I would say 'probably.'

Editor's Note: No, Felix, No. Not another book. This is like literary waterboarding!

To the Reader

Thank you for reading this book. We hope you enjoyed reading it as much as we enjoyed dreaming it up. Please leave an honest book review at Amazon.com or Amazon.ca. Thank you for your support.

The Authors: M.P. Frank and that rascal, Felix the Tomcat

Felix and M.P. Frank website is FelixtheTomcat2022.blog

www.ingramcontent.com/pod-product-compliance
Lightning Source LLC
LaVergne TN
LVHW012047160826
845678LV00014B/2737
9781738816538